Music from a Strange Planet

Stories

Barbara Black

CAITLIN PRESS

Contents

Don't tell me the moon is shining;
show me the glint of light on broken glass.

—Anton Chekhov

Mastering Surface Tension

Bert always wanted a cigarette right when something interesting was happening. Like he could only accommodate change on his own terms. It irritated the hell out of Grace. "Look! Forked lightning!" she'd say. And then instead of looking, he'd reach for his cigs, pop one out, light it, then look.

One June day, Bert climbed the ladder leading to the roof of the house. He had done it many times before, thanks to the exhortations of his loving wife to, for god's sake, do something about the cracked windowpane, the Christmas lights, the leak, the loose shingle. Usually, the supposed defect was a figment of her imagination, which saw decrepitude and disaster lurking in everything. In this case, it was a football-sized hornet nest hanging from the corner of the roof. He lined up the ladder underneath it and climbed to take a look. He liked to at least give the appearance he had done an inspection. The nest appeared inactive. He lit up a cigarette at the top of the ladder and took the opportunity to look into his neighbours' yards.

There was Mr. Gorman, whose first name and profession were a mystery to Bert and whose yard was soulless perfection. Manicured lawn, tightly clipped box hedge, expensive lounges arranged at right angles. It looked like a high-end miniature train set. All it needed was people. But Gorman never entertained anyone in his backyard; he only controlled its growth and staged its possibilities. On the other side was the perma-smile guy, Ed Thompson, who whistled in his garden—mostly vegetables—and was perennially cheerful, as if every day were a pleasant and welcome surprise. His yard was populated with water features, Buddha statues, tiki lights and grandchildren. In the summer his barbecue went nonstop, its primordial charred meat fumes billowing into Bert's domain. Bert was neither precise nor free-form. He was the common man between these two extremes. "You're a good man, Bert, a regular good man," his wife always told him. And his yard was just a plain rectangle of grass.

Bert watched Gorman mowing his impeccable lawn back and forth, back and forth, first in double-wide stripes, then diagonally in a diamond pattern. It looked like something Bert would never achieve in his life. He sucked on his cigarette and exhaled a stream of smoke in the direction of the hornet nest. In the other yard, Ed was picking his tomatoes in that luxuriating Buddha-way of his, admiring each red globe as a miracle of nature, when his cellphone rang. Oddly, at the same time, Bert heard his wife's voice coming from the kitchen.

"Oh, I was up to my neck in blackberries! Pie, jam, you name it." When she laughed, Ed laughed, too. Bert thought it must have been a weird coincidence. He moved up to the ladder's platform with the label that said "Not a Step," trying to spot his wife through the narrow window. His head was now six inches from the nest. A sentry popped out of the entrance, its helmet-like black and white head swivelling to face Bert. It sent out the alarm. The last thing Bert remembered was lying on his back on the sidewalk and seeing a squadron of bald-faced hornets dive-bombing his forehead.

Since then, Bert had been in a so-called vegetative state. By all appearances he was inert, confined to a stark-white hospital room on the fifth floor of St. Francis of Assisi Medical Centre. But, in fact, due to a neural short-circuit in his visual cortex, he was now an insect who roamed a microscopic world of his own creation, a landscape that sometimes resembled a magnified stucco wall, or a dried warped orange peel. Technically, he didn't operate as his human self anymore, but on the other hand, he was free from the constraints of the material world.

Nobody knew of Bert's interior state of being, and had they known, they wouldn't have understood how it came about. Maybe the part of his brain that stored the intense glut of entomological knowledge from seventh grade had suddenly been made accessible. That year, he had spent so much time alone crawling around the forest floor and peering into dirt holes with a magnifying glass that his parents had feared for his sanity. But what he had found in his engagement with the world of earwigs, termites, weevils and stoneflies, cocoons, wasp nests, galls and moults was, above all, kinship. Much of our world is constructed by our brain. Bert's had simply taken it to a whole new level.

Each day, as he lay in the hospital bed, a portal to a new world presented itself, not always pleasant. He didn't think in terms of "days" anymore. Instead, he operated in "intervals." As hospital visitors sat by him, downcast, Bert scuttled through the intervals, knee joints clicking, antennae quivering at odour molecules (passing meal carts), eyes at ground level in his world, which he thought of as "Domain." At first it simply unfolded itself before him, like an opium vision. Later he could actively create the topography and adjust his "attire." If he felt he needed new body parts he switched them in: sculpted elytra, armour, barbed tarsi, an ovipositor (his gender was flexible). Did he feel himself to be a human-sized arthropod or an actual size one? What did it matter? Only the law of dreams applied.

⌒

Driven by guilt and loneliness, Grace visited Bert regularly. The hospital, with all its modern angled glass, made her feel as if she was trapped inside a giant ice crystal. The large room skewed perspective, making Bert look even smaller. From her purse she took out his old black plastic comb and ran it through the limp strands on his head.

"Oh, and Tod insists on staying with me. He's already polished off most of your liquor. They were saying on TV that the Arctic's melting." Her church friend Johanna said global warming was natural, but Grace swore the ocean at the bottom of their street was breaching the high-tide mark already and it worried her. "Do you think we should move, Bert?" The ventilator inhaled as if about to answer.

Tod, their bachelor son, traded hospital shifts with his mother. Transferring his bulk to the undersized chair, he would sit like a giant in kindergarten and read aloud from Bert's favourite book, *How Stuff Works*: "Water has a higher surface tension than most other liquids..." "The tines of the baler intake pick up hay, feeding it into the rollers...." Whether Bert heard him, Tod didn't know, but he felt needed. He wondered why his father had never read to him when he was a kid.

Bert did hear him. In fact, Tod's reading fuelled Bert's excursions into "Domain." And Bert's visions became more detailed, more intense. They had a physiological dimension, too. Regions of his motor cortex and parahippocampal gyrus often flickered like distant lanterns. So distant that no one in the room ever detected them. Thinking, however, remained excruciatingly slow. It could take him two or three days to assemble his body, but his incarnations were not guaranteed successes. "Mayfly," for example, did not go well: he couldn't figure out how to operate his hindwings and kept crashing into the lake. "Water Strider," however, was an interval he revisited several times, revelling in the ideal geometry of his thread-thin legs and the feather-light tiptoe sensation of mastering surface tension. More recently he was learning to detect the pressure waves of objects in his spatial field, a special skill of the much-detested German cockroach. Outwardly, his face and body betrayed nothing of these experiments.

At first, people came with cheery voices and upbeat news, Ed Thompson among them. They crinkled candy wrappers and waved things over his face as if he was a scanner. Gradually, the visits lessened to a smaller circle of friends and family.

Pressure waves. Visitors again. His neighbours the Kilshaws from down the street, and their two young boys.

"He's moving!"

"No, he's not."

"Yes, he is! Just a bit. His temples are twitching."

"I don't see it."

"You missed it. They were."

Meantime, Bert, during his sojourn as a dung beetle, had invented a machine for rolling dung, thereby revolutionizing life for the family Scarabaeidae. He had sensed it was time to ratchet up his invertebrate existence.

Summer unravelled. Grace and Tod dragged the patio chairs back to the shed. Bert's dormant rectangle of grass was revived by the autumn rains. Tod knocked down the old hornet nest with a broomstick, like hitting a human-head piñata. It disintegrated into small ash-like flakes.

As far as his daughter, Lisa, was concerned, Bert was as good as dead. She never visited him. She continued tap-tapping out client reports as she always did in her tiny paper-strewn office at WorkSafe. Her imagination was as feeble as Bert's had been before the accident.

Tod sat on his parents' couch, drinking the remainder of his dad's Johnnie Walker Red, watching the home movie labelled "Shawnigan Lake, 1974." Bert flickered briefly onscreen, waving a blackened pork chop from the barbecue, the lake glistening in the background. Tod had grown closer to Bert since his father had been in the coma, or experiencing "minimal consciousness," as the ICU doctor put it, as if describing a worm. Now Tod spent his days reimagining his childhood as a golden age of father-son ball games, model-making, and fishing expeditions.

The phone rang.

"Mom! Phone's ringing." He rewound to the fishing sequence again so that, in reverse, Bert appeared to lower the cutthroat tail-first through a perfect ring of water and seamlessly guide it back into the depths of the lake. As the answering machine clicked on, Tod shouted, still fixed on the TV, "Someone named Joanne." Grace flew down the stairs and lifted the receiver.

Two weeks after Bert's accident, Grace started attending the First Memorial Church of Faith, which Johanna had suggested the day she had touched Grace's hand so sympathetically and recommended that Grace read the Book of Job. Grace found its endless litany of disaster horrifying but was too polite to say so. Now when she visited Bert, she keened prayers over him with evangelical fervour: "Oh Lord, fill this man with your divine spirit, raise him up to life to see once again the glory of Creation!" In the past, the closest she ever got to religion was when she and Bert first met in 1960 and made out in Saint Luke's churchyard, knocking over a small stone cross, which they hauled off as a souvenir, Grace shouting to the moon, "Forgive me, Mr. Jesus!" The cross still stands crookedly in the shade garden of their backyard, guarding the grave of their first dog, Ripley. She was beginning to think that what made you a certain kind of person depended largely on what kind of person the *other* person in your life thought you were.

More intervals passed. Without ongoing cues about his body, Bert's conception of himself as human had vanished. As Grace grew weary of her inert husband, he was enjoying the glory of his own creation. Mating paraphernalia and positions occupied him for hours and hours: the ideal spermatophore transfer method, or if he preferred to be in a higher order, length of the endophallus, tarsi to grip the smooth backs of females, grasping position, etcetera. Way back, while his schoolmates were ogling *Playboy* centrefolds, Bert the twelve-year-old was diving into the mechanics of invertebrate copulation, which were to him more erotic than the mechanics of human coitus.

Grace came. He felt the pressure wave. And maybe another thicker density beside her, he wasn't sure. She dragged the chair closer, making the rubber ends on the chair legs squeal, causing his landscape to temporarily collapse. "Bert, I've met someone. At church." He had no idea how many intervals it had been since his fall. "I thought I should tell you." If he'd been able to light up a cigarette, he would have. Instead, he spread his wings wide to listen.

"I just want you to know how much I still love you," she said, parting his hair with the black comb. "Even though..." her voice trailed off. She knew you could never really replace one love with another; you could only displace the original, push it to the back of the drawer where the old underwear languishes. She stared at Bert, distressed that he looked so otherworldly, like an alien version of himself.

As that long-ago twelve-year-old, Bert imagined that the woman he would fall in love with would be as dainty as the green lacewing, his favourite nocturnal insect. *Chrysopa*—golden eyes. He had imagined the vibrations of his mating song travelling from his body down into the ground upon which she would stand before him.

Grace continued to pour forth reasons for abandoning him. But her voice started to feel prickly, different than it was in the past, like tiny barbs puncturing his abdomen. The longer she spoke, the less he could understand. Her words became sound-wave shapes, percussive vocalizations, swirling moans, like a floor polisher making its way down a long, narrowing hallway.

"Tod and Lisa and I will all be here with you in the room...." She whispered a fervent prayer, patted his hand and left.

Bert snapped his wings back smartly, groomed his antennae, and re-entered "Domain." On the other side of the white hills—no, he had changed them to ochre now—his new mate was waiting.

Darkling Beetle

The glasses, oh god, the glasses. "Honey," I said, "are you sure you want those pointy ones? It's your first day of grade three."

"Yeah," she said.

"These ones that look like owl eyes?"

"Yeah."

"What about these, sweetie? They're blue and there's a pretty pattern on the side."

"I don't like those."

So we bought the pointy ones and the grade three kids called her Mrs. Owl. She cried and cried for an hour after school in her room, but the next day she still wore those awful glasses. It was as if ugliness was her identity. As if, unlike the other kids, she didn't even make a distinction between ugliness and beauty; it was all the same continuum. Wherever she went, a little trail of mockery followed behind. But off she would go into her geeky girl land and she always found her way home, navigating the perilous forest of an awkward childhood.

Two weeks before Halloween, I'm trying to find the perfect costume for her. It's seven o'clock and Cora's in her room. I knock gently. "Sweetie, I've just found a great outfit for you!"

She opens the door. "What?"

"Look, Beauty from *Beauty and the Beast*."

She doesn't look. She goes back to her Kindle, swiping to the next page.

"Sweetie, I can make it for you. You'll look so pretty!"

No. She is determined to revel in her homeliness. It's not my fault she didn't get my family's good looks. She shrinks her little self into the Kindle screen, like a retreating genie willing itself back into the lamp.

When I go back to the living room, my husband looks over his *Forbes* magazine with his second set of eyes on his forehead and says, "Listen to this. It's a quote from some billionaire designer guy: 'Glasses protect your soul from others.'" He loves those profound kinds of statements, like just by reading them he can change the world.

All week I pore over magazines at the supermarket looking for a different costume. No beauties. *Martha Stewart* has it: a sorceress (but not a warty one). Scary but elegant, with a crystal ball and a fabulous hat. I buy all the listed supplies. I stay up late making it in secret, after editing policy briefs, cursing the sewing machine. When I get to bed, my husband is still reading. He puts down his *New Yorker*. "Have you heard of the furries?" he says. I can see the glow in the back of his eyes at yet another discovery of some weird fringe element of society. "They go to conventions dressed up like wolves and bunnies and flamingos so they can have sex!"

"Uh, why?"

"Apparently, they feel more comfortable as animals, not humans. Listen to this: 'Yiff' means sex and 'yiffy' means horny. Amazing." He shows me a photo of a burly guy dressed as a warthog.

"Yes, amazing."

On Saturday morning after pancakes I show Cora the costume. "Close your eyes. Now open."

She looks as if she's about to get a vaccination. Her body stiffens and there's a small terror trapped in her face. "I don't want to be anything *people!*" she shouts and runs to her bedroom.

"Stop bullying her," my husband says.

"I'm not bullying her."

"Yes, you are. You're trying to be the mother you wanted to have but didn't."

"No, I'm not. She just needs a little self-esteem boost."

In response, my husband stirs his tea like a disgruntled percussionist assaulting a triangle.

Finally, no more sounds come from her room. *She's probably forgotten.* I peek in and she's perched on her bed. She's crying silently like a paralyzed person, stiff, no movement in her face, tears streaming like rain on the windows of an abandoned house. "Cora. It's okay if you don't like it." She's still in the distant land that I'm never invited into. I sit on the end of the bed. Children are a mystery, a bundle of your genes and something else that is not quite you.

Suddenly her face clears. "Mom, I want to go as a darkling beetle. They're beautiful."

"A... what?"

"A darkling beetle. They're one of the most important beetle families in the world. *Eleodes carbonarius.* They're reddish black with ridges on their back and they have hooked legs. They can spray chemicals at you if you scare them. And they have antennae with little knobs."

"Okay, Sweetie. I can do that. No problem." I could already see her hunched in a corner of the party, abandoned by her classmates who chose to be Disney characters, bunnies and superheroes.

"Thanks, Mom." She wraps her arms around my neck and presses her owl glasses into my cheek.

⌒

We go together to pick out the fabric. She's very particular about the nap and texture, and its weight, how it will sit on her body. She pores over rolls like a Talmudic scholar, finally choosing "the brown shimmery one." We buy wire for the antennae, which has to be the right thickness, and a different fabric than the carapace. She's worried that her face will look too human. The store clerk clears her throat and suggests that makeup will help.

My husband brings home a life-sized Egyptian mummy with glowing eye sockets to prop by the door. I tell him the poor kiddies will be scared out of their wits.

"There's something to be said for that, honey-bun." He pinches my bum.

⌒

I start working on the costume four days before Halloween, after Cora has gone to bed so she doesn't hear my swearing. I screw up my first try on the carapace and have to start all over again. I can't figure out how to space the legs or how to do the joints as she wants, never mind how to make those pesky little hooks on the feet.

Two days before Halloween, I want to quit. I want a pretty daughter who plays with dolls and wears pink T-shirts and doesn't have to wear glasses. I put my head down and weep all over the damn beetle cloth. It does have an interesting texture. I run my fingers along the corduroy ridges. She made a perfect choice. I wipe my nose. I hold up the costume. It's okay. I did the legs right—six, as Cora ordered. I run my hands through the strips of velveteen she chose for the antennae, remembering the look on the clerk's face at Fabricland as Cora had unfurled the roll and inspected it.

I finish the darkling beetle at one in the morning. I'm so pleased with myself I stay up and drink half a bottle of Bordeaux, then creep upstairs. My husband is lying on the bed, dressed as a rabbit, with a coy smile on his face, his paws smoothing down his white fur. Draped across my side of the bed is a plushy red fox costume with a gigantic bow on it. It's gorgeous.

⟶

At the first house, I stand at the bottom of the steps in the dark. My husband, the rabbit, is back home giving out treats. Cora knocks softly on the neighbour's door, adjusting her glasses and antennae.

"Look! We've got a June bug on our doorstep!"

"No. I'm a darkling beetle."

"Oh. That's really cool, Miss Beetle. Do you eat candy?"

"No. I eat old leaves and rotten wood."

In that moment, something strange and beautiful flies from my heart like the last bat from the cave.

Night People

It's two in the morning. Two houses are lit up in a town of sleepers. In one there is a man with a stiff neck gluing together the wing assembly of a model airplane. He bends his head down over the model to see closer, then sits up and stretches his neck, massaging it with his right hand. In the other house there is a woman, small-boned and lithe, perched on a stool in her kitchen eating olives lined up on a plate. She picks up each one, holds it to the light, then sucks out the pimento filling. Each occupant is enveloped in the silence of early morning, yet not embraced enough by it to be sleeping. The man is awake because he *won't* sleep. The woman is awake because she can't sleep.

Somewhere in the neighbourhood there is a rabid raccoon.

The man used to be a dentist. The woman used to be an acrobat. When she was young, and a mistress of the unity of movement, the woman could bend and flex her body, do the splits, fly from a trapeze, smile upside down in a back bend. Today's circuses don't want forty-year-old performers. She resists sleep because she keeps dreaming acrobatic accidents: a quivering knee whose uncontrolled vibrations spread to the calf, to the toes, translating into a quiver in the high wire and a creeping fraction of doubt. She never falls in the dreams but wakes at the point where her body becomes a composite of parts and can no longer be commanded by her mind.

The man, unaware of the woman eating olives just ten houses away, holds the plane's horizontal stabilizer in his fingers. Northrop P-61 Black Widow. As a boy, he always wanted to build the night bomber but never had, and he can't remember why. Lately, he can barely remember anything—at least, no details. Instead, his memory is a blur of associations and emotions with a noticeable breakdown in sequence and logic. This disturbs him. For five weeks (he documented it on the calendar) his sleep had been rife with unsettling dreams, so he tries his best not to sleep. His hand shakes as he inserts the stabilizer into the wing assembly. Rubbing the glue off his fingertips, he glances over the assembly instructions to plan his next move.

In his most recent dream, he was walking down a sandy beach to the shore. When he stepped into the sea, his foot dissolved. The deeper he went, the more of his body dissolved. He knew less and less who he was or what he was. He felt he was a collection of blood vessels, muscles and bones undergoing a chemical merger with a liquid. He deemed this to be a highly irregular dream for a former dentist. As a result, he willed himself to stop sleeping.

Sleep deprived, he takes solace in the slow assemblage of component parts—anything to stop the threat of merging. He lays out the remaining pieces for his model and feels momentarily overwhelmed, rubs the back of his neck. The best way to do it is to proceed part by part, being careful not to inhale too much epoxy. Glue fumes only exacerbate his condition. He is not accustomed to euphoria and distrusts it. He glances over the instructions. The nose gear. "Install using four large wood screws provided." They should have said *tiny* wood screws. His hand shakes too much as he tries to get the first screw in the mounting rails. He can feel his concentration flagging. His ability to carry out minutely measured movements, like a trainer in a flea circus, is greatly diminished. He can't locate his hands in space. He gives up.

Unlike the woman, he knows about the raccoon because he is the one who started feeding it at night. It seems especially fond of olives.

⌐

The woman has run out of olives. She sits in front of her plate, with its tiny pools of vinegar, and sucks her teeth, unsure how to fill the remaining hours of darkness. She decides to go to the all-night store for more olives. She puts her coat on over her nightgown and goes out the front door. The rabid raccoon is foraging in the compost pile in her backyard, but she doesn't know this. She tests the doorknob twice to make sure it's locked behind her, the first time out of habit, the second a forced coalition between mind and fingers. The night air smells faintly of the coffee grounds the raccoon has stirred up.

She walks down the sidewalk in a straight line as if walking a tightrope. The rest of the town sleeps behind bevelled doors. It is an unfriendly small town. People stay locked up in themselves. They require small accidents to be shocked into interest, and even then, their curiosity is only a way of confirming the safety of their own lives. The woman has lived here for a month and has met no one, only passing coats filled with people.

The route to the store, three blocks west of her house, will take her past the man's house. She has underestimated the chill and picks up her pace to keep warm. When she passes the man's house, he is inside struggling to attach the radar aerials on the side of the fuselage. When she reaches the store, the pale young man with vacant eyes says they're out of olives. "Nope. None," he intones blandly.

After four years of working nights in the all-night store and seeing the assortment of foods which that strange breed, the night people, buy for countering insomnia, nothing surprises him. Olives merely join a long buffet table in his mind crowded with popcorn, ice cream, chocolate bars, Cheezies, smoked oysters, Kraft dinner, beef jerky and canned fruit cocktail. He's learned not to look night people in the eye since they seize upon any opportunity to launch into their woeful tales of sleeplessness.

This time, however, curious at the way the woman mourns on tiptoes at the pickle shelf, or vaguely intrigued by the way she moves so consciously through space, or maybe because his late-night movie has just ended, he breaks his own rule and says, "Some guy comes in at, like, three a.m. every Friday and buys them all." It's Saturday. The woman thanks him sadly and tightrope-walks her way out the front door.

⤳

By now, it's 2:30 a.m. Even the town dogs, their limbic brains lulled by darkness, are asleep. The woman doubts that anybody in this town suffers from insomnia and considers them lucky. She walks like steam spilling down the street, thinking of the taste of green olives. Olives with pimento, olives with garlic, olives with feta, Manzanilla olives. It unsettles her that an unknown person in town should share her snack food idiosyncrasy.

The man is on his front steps holding a jar of Manzanilla olives. The raccoon prefers these. It rolls each one between its paws before eating it. It usually appears about this time, which makes him glad since this is exactly the time his attention starts to wane. He sees the animal emerge from the shrubbery. It's behaving strangely tonight— or maybe it isn't the same raccoon.

The woman is a block away. From a distance she can see the man as he leans forward and feeds what she thinks is a very fat cat. As she nears, she realizes it's a raccoon. It's bobbing its head and scuttling in counter-clockwise circles as if trying to unwind itself. It seems perplexed by its own movements. The body twitches first, the brain interprets after the fact, as if it's forgotten its own being and is trying on all identities, flipping through the animal kingdom like a Rolodex.

It's not interested in whatever the man is feeding it.

She's one house away when the man, who has given up, turns to go back inside. As he reaches for the doorknob, the animal hunches down on its hips, ready to launch an attack. She rushes toward his driveway and by blurting, "Watch out!" is able to give him a fraction of a second to react. He drops the jar of olives on the front steps, which startles the raccoon enough to send it lumbering away. The woman rushes up. There's a strong smell of brine in the air. The two of them stand dumbly watching the animal's retreat. Her white nightgown is poking out of her coat. He's wearing sweatpants and a pair of slippers that look as if they've been chewed by a dog. She notices his fingertips are dirty and coated with something.

"You feed it olives?" she says, observing the scattered contents of the broken jar. She holds her coat lapels together.

He looks down at his masticated slippers, then raises his head, careful not to look her right in the eye. "He seems to like them. Or, uh, used to."

A sleepy silence ensues. Their bodies start to relax.

"You're walking at night?" he asks, kindly, pulling up his saggy pajama bottoms.

"Can't sleep."

"Welcome to the club."

He glances at his feet again. "Come in and get warm," he says, stepping over the glass. He waves her inside without waiting for her reply, in the way that sleep-deprived people forget social graces. She follows across the threshold like a hypnotized subject. It smells of glue. On what appears to be the dining room table is a chaotic mess of plastic bits, glue tubes, paint jars, papers and a black model airplane complete with model machine guns, with the name "Moonlight Serenade" on the body. He shows her to a flowery armchair in the living room.

"Sit down and I'll make some coffee. Or would you, uh, prefer a cocktail?"

Her petite frame in the chair makes her look like a tiny creature in a field of daisies. "Could you make a martini?"

He nods yes.

"Gin. With an—"

"Got it."

They sit in the living room with their tinkling glasses, she in her nightie and he in his makeshift pajamas, as if they both aren't in their sleepwear. Or maybe it's that much easier because they are in their sleepwear; it precludes the usual pretences. For a moment she chides herself for entering the house of a stranger (in her nightie!), but doesn't have the energy to leave. An odd, scratchy electronic orchestra plays from a portable stereo on a side table.

"This music. It's... interesting."

"Graeme Revell, *The Insect Musicians*. He's a genius. Scores for, uh, movies now. The electronic samples are field recordings—wind, birds, water, bugs. Mostly bugs. And then he built the, uh, music around it. It holds my brain together. For a while anyway."

"It makes me feel itchy."

He smiles. He has good teeth.

"Is that the Black Widow?" she asks, glancing at the work table.

"How did you know that?"

"My father was a US Air Force mechanic. He loved that plane. There were pictures of it all over our garage. I think he loved it more than our mother."

"Northrop P-61. Night raider. Could fly at forty-five hundred feet. Good for acrobatics." He yawns audibly. "Couldn't get the nose gear screwed in."

She goes to the table and picks it up. "My brother was crazy about model airplanes. Couldn't stop talking about them. The whole ceiling in his bedroom was full of them: Mustangs, Spitfires, Messerschmitts. He must have read every book in the library on the Second World War." When she turns around, the man is asleep. She sits back down in her chair, folds and unfolds her hands in her lap, stares at his face, the dark rings under his eyes. The cycling chirps and rasping drones from the CD are like the inner workings of a cell made audible. She could leave at this point, with the man asleep on his own couch, but her body seems finally to have given up its balancing act against gravity. After two minutes she falls asleep in the armchair, her left arm dangling over the side, her coat collar open to reveal the embroidered yoke of her white nightie. It's 3:07 a.m.

Hot July Day

Two girls stand together on the roadside. The taller one, Jordan, has thick brown hair and eyes with a crow-like intensity. Each event for her represents an opportunity. The shorter girl, Dee, looks unsure of herself, impressionable. What does the tall girl value in her? The gift of camouflage.

Several hearses had just driven by, gleaming black on a hot July day, the heat wave of 1969. A local teenager had shot every member of his extended family, except his identical twin. As the hearses passed, the neighbourhood children sucked on their homemade popsicles, imagining the shiny coffins inside. As engrossing as watching an LP slip round and round on the turntable, but emitting no sounds, only a groove being scratched, seminal memories in the making.

A third girl, very small for her age, stands on the porch of her nearby house, watching the procession from afar. She is not allowed to go and rubberneck at anything, especially funerals. Her father's a police officer. She has no popsicle. She hunches in her hand-me-down summer shift. Her face is shrew-like, with a tense expression as if her skin is too tight. The distinct air of the outcast.

Jordan has taunted this girl, Louise, and on occasion made her cry. All three girls were in the same grade five class together that year. It was Jordan who came up with the nickname "Midge," not the girl's name but short for "midget."

Cottonwood sap fills the air with sticky sweetness. Or is it too late for cottonwood sap? *Something* smells sweet and cloying. It's surprising that lately no fire engines have whizzed past on their way to the canyon to rescue the reckless and the dispossessed who swirl round and round in the whirlpools. And there is no one up in the rifle range shooting clay pigeons. Only the sound of twirling sprinklers—*sheet-sheet-sheet*—and children's cries as their bare feet slap the wet grass.

This funeral procession was a special event in a town where nothing happened, and it gave Jordan an idea, which she planned meticulously in her head while licking her popsicle right down to the stick without any melted bits falling off.

The next day Jordan tracked Louise to the corner store.

"Pretty good story you wrote in English class. I remember it. You copied it, didn't you?" She squinted at Louise, who was carrying a bag containing sanitary napkins. Louise pressed her lips together. As the daughter of a cop, she had been brought up to never tell a lie. The consequences were having your mouth washed out with soap, or worse. Usually worse now that her mother was gone. Jordan crossed in front of Louise and walked backwards. "So? Did you? I saw you in the library. You were copying. You were writing it all down. Isn't that illegal?"

"It's my story," Louise said without looking Jordan in the eyes.

"Ooooh. Okay. I be-lieeeve you. You're a genius." Jordan stabbed at her own head. "If I only had a brain. Hey, I wanna learn how to write a story, too. So, can you teach me?"

"Well...."

"Oh, c'mon. How about tomorrow?"

⌐

They met in the community hall youth room after the three days Louise needed to study every book in the library about how to write a story. She memorized all the best points and painstakingly copied out instructions that she gave to Jordan on note cards. They sat in the dim room where it was almost too cool for bare arms and legs, in the vague tang of stale sweat left over from teen dances. The two of them seemed to get along. Jordan started affectionately calling Louise "genius," which Louise knew was code for "stupid," but she didn't care. This was the closest thing to a friend she had ever had. They forged a tentative alliance.

⌐

It was one of those old-fashioned baby buggies, slightly archaic, almost gothic, with a fabric hood and four large rubber wheels. It had been sitting in the back of the garage since Jordan's little brother had disappeared, the fabric accumulating random rosettes of mold. Even his blanket was still in there, spread out as if waiting, its jolly ducks and farm animals fading into vagueness like that moment the TV tube dies.

Jordan waited till her mom staggered up the stairs for her late afternoon "nap," then yanked the buggy out. She gave it a few wipes with a rag and it smelled okay. Her accomplice, Dee, stood by, mesmerized by the precision of the tall girl's every movement. With fervent single-mindedness, Jordan maneuvered the buggy out of the garage.

"Okay. We got ourselves a hearse. Let's go."

Down in the canyon, white-limbed boys leapt awkwardly into the churning water hoping to be transformed into men. Girls preferred a different sort of play.

Was it a summer day to remember? To children, of course not. Children don't spend their time remembering things. Their brains, at this point, are elastic receptacles of pure experience. What will imprint the day as memorable will depend on one of two emotions marking it: joy or trauma.

The two girls called at Louise's house, then all three walked toward "The Bush," as it was known then, an adult-free space where imagination ran free, where wildness and abandonment were embraced or unleashed, where panties were found flung under shrubs, and patches of ground were singed by furtive campfires. Where the big kids sat around on old ripped-up car seats, holding secret meetings in the night, drinking beer stolen from their parents.

"Everyone says Wendy didn't drown in the canyon. Some pervert raped her and buried her in the Bush. We could be walking on her bones right now."

Louise looked down at her feet just to check.

Dee crossed her arms against her body. "Stop it, Jordan. You're scaring me. I wanna go home."

Jordan flicked her hand in Dee's face.

Louise thought the Bush did not smell like summer. It smelled mushroomy, like fall, like the smell of her father's armpits when he yelled at her. But she didn't say this out loud.

Jordan bumped the buggy along the narrow path and outlined her vision for what should take place. The buggy was the hearse. Louise would be the dead baby. Dee would be the silent stoic father. Jordan (since she had boobs, sort of) would be the mother grieving for her lost one, leading him/her (they decided on her) to her tiny grave. Louise objected to being the baby just because she was small. She wanted to be the mother. Dee offered her the role of the father, but Jordan shot her a sharp look and insisted the casting was perfect.

"Get in the buggy, Midgie. We'll cover you with the blanket." Louise started to cry. "You can't cry! You're dead. Remember? This is the best role in the whole story! Get in." Louise clambered into the buggy unsteadily. She tried to lie down but she was a bit too big, so she had to hang her feet off the end. Jordan pushed the buggy to the "cemetery," snapping off branches as the path narrowed. Dee attempted some flat dialogue as the grieving father, but Jordan ignored her. When they reached a small clearing littered with cigarette butts, Jordan—with strange facial expressions—instructed Dee to go and find a square rock to be the grave marker. Louise began to be afraid that they might bury her. But not in a box like her mother was. She was trying to come up with a lie to get out of the buggy, but the strict truth edict of her upbringing failed her.

"Now. Midgie. I have to change you—well, your *body*—before we put you in the ground. This is the way it's done. Sit up! Arms up!" She grabbed the bottom of Louise's cotton dress and pulled it off. Louise acquiesced. "See. You're perfect for the role. No titties. Now take off your underwear, cuz babies can't go to heaven wearing underwear." Louise didn't want to, but the way Jordan was glaring at her, she obeyed. She said she was cold. Jordan gave her the tiny blanket but held Louise's clothes tightly under her arm. "Okay, Louise. Close your eyes tight. Ashes for ashes. Till death do its part, we bury this poor child," Jordan said solemnly. "Now I'm the mother, so I have to go and put on my special mourning clothes for the funeral. Just wait a second. Stay dead." Jordan disappeared down an embankment.

Louise waited frozen in position in the old buggy, clutching the baby blanket. She was confused. Wasn't the funeral *before* the burial? That's how she remembered it. A volley of shots rang out from the rifle range. It was getting late to be shooting. After a few minutes she thought maybe she should try to get out, but Jordan still had her clothes. Mosquitoes whined around her ears, trying to get blood. Her father said it was the females, not the males, who bite because they need blood for their young. Knowing her father, she suspected this was a lie. It was men who stabbed and hunted and shot things. He was going to blow up if she was late for dinner. She heard twigs snapping in the opposite direction and was worried that someone was coming and would see her. No one came.

The sun dropped down into the green-black woods. Robins started their evening song. A chill rose up from the ground. She felt the way you feel when you jump into a lake that's too cold and you can never get warm again. She got out of the buggy and hid in the bushes until what she thought was dinnertime. Her teeth were chattering. Sirens whined in the distance, but they didn't come for her. She didn't cry. When she was sure that everybody in the neighbourhood was inside, she ran all the way home naked, through the back lanes and snuck in the back door. She put on fresh clothes from the laundry pile on the dryer, and got to dinner just a few seconds late.

She did not sit across from her older brother. She sat where her mother used to sit, at the end of the table opposite her father. Just as her father opened his mouth to yell at her, she drew herself upright and looked him in the eye: "I was at the library." With these words it was as if the entire room—dining table, chairs, sideboard—shifted on its axis and she was no longer the least important person at the table.

Belly-Deep in White Clover

He saw the entry point of the bullet through the chest, into the heart region, a small jolt where life narrowed to a pinpoint, then vanished. For a second, he felt the impact on his own body. It was a juvenile male porcupine, about three months old, likely already foraging on its own with the mother nearby. He had never done a porcupine mount and he wasn't going to start now. He picked up his magnifying glass. There were blowfly eggs embedded in the wound. He tweezed them out. And a .22 long rifle bullet.

His name was Johns. He'd lived alone out here in the Bulkley-Nechako for thirty-one years. He was himself a bit porcupine-like: hunched, prickly, solitary, nocturnal. Hardly anybody in the valley knew him anymore, and the few who did kept their distance. His last friend, Bjørn Bulldog Torske, a renowned trapper in the area, died eleven years ago of septicemia. Johns believed in the idea of will and knew the consequences of the loss of it, which his friend had suffered the last years of his life. You had to stick with something to keep going.

Taxidermy was a dead art. These days you could buy preformed idiot polyurethane forms straight out of a catalogue. Made every animal look the same. He glanced at his sandpipers with their slender beaks, posed in artificial salt pools facing a waveless sea. He still constructed his own armatures and recreated each animal's physique with excelsior and clay. But no one was interested in taxidermy anymore. His commissions had dwindled to restorations of moth-eaten martens and herons and time-consuming dioramas of impossible species combinations for an eccentric collector named Brackdale, who'd bought seventeen lots of taxidermied specimens from the now defunct Tweedsmuir Museum of Natural History. Johns had been methodically remolding a cougar's nose from this collection when some local, with a sharp rap on the door, dropped the porcupine at his back doorstep. Probably shot by those idiots who charge through the woods like mercenaries, slaughtering animals for fun. Way back when, he would have disposed of it in the woods, but instead he carried it gingerly, with gloves, bagged it, and laid it out whole in the mammal freezer.

Johns was seventy-nine now, and passed the time with taxidermy, eating, sleeping and reading model train magazines from the sixties. In the past, he'd listened to the radio, and later to a few old albums. Famous steam and diesel locomotives: *Audio Fidelity, The Sounds of a Vanishing Era.* Or Tennessee Ernie Ford singing "Shenandoah," which sounded to him like a yearning that lasts clear into eternity. Then one day, music felt unnecessary to living. He stopped listening to it altogether, preferring the natural melody of place and time. He stopped hunting, too. Kill or be killed—he was no longer afraid of the latter prospect. He had been fixed in the sights of a black bear sow more than once.

⌐

The day after someone dropped off the juvenile quarry, an adult porcupine appeared at the back gate. The mother, he thought. She sat staring at Johns' house. As night fell, she became a silhouette, like a small dusk-lit statue in an overgrown garden. He stood at the window watching her while he rolled a cigarette. He didn't smoke anymore, just kept the cigarettes in his pocket or left them dotted around the house, random white scats that marked his thoughts. The porcupine appeared the next evening, too, and the next. A vigil. Females have only one offspring per year. He didn't believe in feeding wild animals, but he kept leaving her a bit of leftover corncob, and she ate it all. If an animal can mourn, that probably means it can feel some kind of affection. He wasn't sure.

The fourth evening, she was there again. He went out in his blue work coveralls. With an outstretched hand, he approached her with another cob. They were placid animals unless provoked. She regarded him with her shiny brown-black eyes and moved forward to accept it, her paws soft and textured. As she gnawed the kernels with her square red teeth, she made a squeaky childlike sound. The noise surprised him. It was somewhat endearing. When finished, she placed the cob on the ground, waddled away a few feet and turned, as if beckoning him to follow her, which he did, his hunched figure a larger version of her own. They crossed the threshold between his property line and the distant woods.

Past the old well she led him with her loping walk, past the rusty tractor skeleton and the disintegrated smokehouse into taller grass that led to the spruce grove up the hill. Sweeping along the forest floor, the porcupine seemed to know exactly where she was going: a stand of red alders along Takleult Creek and more specifically, one festooned with catkins that looked as if it could hardly support her weight. Johns stood watching her shinny up. It was just past dusk and the scented air floated down, resinous from the lodgepole pines. The drought had weakened them, brought the bark beetles that would eat them from the inside out. Johns was conversant with the valley's flora and fauna, but he sensed there was an entire language to it that was beyond him. He pulled out his tobacco pouch and filled a cigarette paper, rolled it, ran it across his tongue, then underneath his nose.

Put it in his pocket. The pine resin put him in mind of his old friend Bjørn and his house tucked into a sun-dotted pine grove. Bjørn, blasting out his front door the day he showed Johns his new dog, Jake, the husky–border collie cross. Bjørn had built it a doghouse, a miniature Norwegian farmhouse, painted red. The day Johns had stopped using a gun was the day he'd had to shoot Bjørn's beloved old orphaned dog.

He went home, puzzled as to why the porcupine had led him to her perch. He didn't mind the walk, though. It'd been a long time since he'd wandered beyond his own nine acres.

Supper was steak and canned peas. He sat outside in his beaver-skin chair while the stars made bright pinpricks in the darkness. A northern saw-whet owl called escalating staccato pitches that sounded like notes from a small wooden flute. He spent the remaining night hours working on a timber wolf restoration, replacing the incorrect eyes and softening the decades-old face by moistening the lips and applying putty so the mouth could be more relaxed and natural. The old boy looked more himself by the hour.

A sliver of morning sun showed behind Miligit Peak, as pink as new skin. It was something neither Johns nor the porcupine saw often, being the nocturnal types. When the first rays of light made the lamp redundant, Johns headed for bed. Up with the sunset, down with the dawn. Past the mounted heads of moose and bighorn sheep, his prized saw-whet owl and the red-throated loon, he reinserted himself into the imprint of his body on the sheets.

⁓

Johns began to look forward to evenings with her. Lydia, he had started calling her. He had never named an animal. Sometimes she came down to the gate, and once when he'd left his back door ajar, she'd wandered into his mudroom and chewed one of his boots. Salt was her drug. On other occasions he had to seek her out. If they started early and there was still enough light, he brought along a small art book and sketched her. It was easy. She didn't move very fast. Then again, neither did he.

One Sunday evening, about a month after Lydia started visiting, he stepped outside. There was a weight to the night air on these mid-July days. It seemed a layer of heat a few feet above the ground did not dissipate but lay suspended there day after day. He inhaled and let the sky draw him upwards. His spine stretched, restoring a little of his height and, with it, a cleanness in his soul.

Today Lydia wasn't at the gate or tumbling down through the grass to greet him. He walked up Sleeman's Hill, where he'd seen her lingering before. Fire hazard was high. He could feel it in the parched trees. The forest was restlessly alive. He followed her trail of debarked trees from previous winters. There was a site littered with nipped twigs. He looked high up into her favoured pine, but she wasn't there. Not tonight. He headed west over the hill to where the little light remaining illuminated the meadow.

Johns finally located her foraging on an open slope, belly-deep in white clover and wild grass. The cascade of blonder hairs on her back showed up in the dusk light. He moved within three hundred feet of her, squatting down in the grass. Out of curiosity he sampled a clover flower himself. Sweet, a hint of licorice and nectar. It was eating of the very landscape in which they lived, moved, defecated, died. He imagined that to her, he was more a smell or a presence, since her eyes wouldn't be all that good. Given his poor hygiene, he supposed he made a distinct impression. As if reading his thoughts, Lydia lifted her head. His scent must have slipped down to the hollow where she was feeding. He didn't always seek to be right next to her; he didn't believe in domesticating wildlife. But on several closer occasions, they had made direct eye contact. In taxidermy if he didn't get the eye contact right it was failure. The eyes are where the feeling of life resides.

Before hard darkness fell, he said goodbye to Lydia and descended back to the house, his shadow tracking him in moonlight.

⤳

The only good thing about the collector's commission was the money. As soon as Johns had clinched the deal, he'd ordered a double bed made from red oak, which would be delivered on the tenth of August. In the meantime, he cursed the absurdity of the project. An otter, for example, would never encounter a rattlesnake. He had tried to tell the old bugger they were from different habitats. But Brackdale only said, "You've got a free hand. Coyotes and skunks playing poker if you like, herons wearing kimonos, just none of that godawful scientific stuff." What Johns hated about this fantasy taxidermy was it took away the animal's own story. Taxidermy's real calling was to honour it.

In the company of rearing grizzlies and grazing mule deer, amidst the silent artificial tongues of the bobcat, the fox and the badger, he worked on the commission till dawn, intermittently swearing.

⤳

Once there'd been a few homesteads dotting these meadows and valleys, old houses and outbuildings whose crumbling frames had long ago collapsed back into the land. The porcupines, and there had always been porcupines, had chewed every last fence post, salty axe handle, gun butt and moldering leather boot, rendering them back to their timber and animal origins. People were generally not thankful for this service.

Back of Johns' place to the south was the denuded ridge, which put him in mind of a damaged hide that would only grow back patchily and unbeautiful, if at all. His friend Bjørn had had a small timber licence. But even he had been against wholesale clear-cuts. In the last few years, with more and larger cutblocks, most of the original valley folks had defected. Animals, too. Logging left isolated habitats here and there. The land had to wait for succession growth to put itself back together. Johns likely wouldn't be around to see that. As for the untouched areas, they still held forth a certain beauty.

End of July. A cloudy night, the horizon orange from a distant forest fire, an odour of ash and cinders assaulting the nostrils. Unseen scent trails streaked over the ground. Routes crisscrossed, overlapped, circled back, betraying those who had made them. Lydia and Johns had ventured deeper into the woods tonight, farther than they'd ever gone. She seemed agitated or excited, he was not sure which. Johns had stopped to adjust his boot laces and lost track of her so had headed back home toward the meadow where it was easier to see in the low light.

Maybe she was heading away from the wood smoke. The beetled pines were an ideal fuel. Could keep a fire going for days. In the east, the molten colour glowed steadily, like an unresolved sunset. Johns had been walking for a few minutes when he noticed something in the air flowing down from the hill. A stink. A defense bomb to warn predators. He raced back up the hill, waving his arms like a cattle herder, with crazed shouts of "Hep! Huh!" which were answered by an ungodly shriek.

After a frantic charge through the trees, he reached Lydia. Some animal had ambushed her. She lay on the ground under a spruce, her neck broken and a few slashes to her face. Quills everywhere. Fisher. This was their method. Tree the porcupine and cause a fall, then eat the whole animal, leaving only a hide. Johns had mounted a few fishers. They had retractable claws. The animal had taken one swipe into Lydia's belly before Johns had scared it off. He knelt beside her. The fisher screamed far-off like a girl being murdered in the woods. He tasted the tang of blood in his own mouth. Some viscera had spilled out of Lydia's chest. He lifted and carefully folded it back in. She was still warm. In her eyes, nothing. He slid his jacket under her back as best he could and sat cradling her, letting the odd quill pierce his arms. The trees were still; the air hung thick and sooty, and for the first time in weeks the night did not feel alive.

Under threat of darkness, he carried her home.

Against his usual practice, he put on Ernie Ford. "Oh, Shenandoah." Where the fur was torn, he sutured up Lydia's belly, then removed her hide. He couldn't bear to dispose of her. Without fur, her body looked like an infant cadaver, vulnerable and new. He put her in the specimen freezer, preserved in alcohol. Next to the juvenile porcupine, which may or may not have been hers. He took a hand-rolled cigarette out of his coveralls, ran it slowly back and forth under his nose and put it down on the counter.

She had already lost several hundred quills in the attack. He removed over two hundred more from the hide, placing them in an old jar on the windowsill for safekeeping. He fleshed, degreased and washed the hide. Once it had dried, he took particular care brushing out her thick fur. Out of habit, he started his usual armature from wrapped excelsior. But he changed his mind. He wanted the body to be pliable. Wire joints for her legs and a soft filler for her body. A "soft" mount, it was called. Only her head would require a hard mold. The paws would be filled with clay. He went through the trays of spare glass eyes. Birds: standard pupil, large pupil, pinpoint pupil, two-colour blended. Reptiles (not many). Mammals: oval pupil, round pupil, slit pupil. Only one suitable pair, small, dark and shiny like pokeweed berries, twelve millimetres, which he put aside.

He made her soft and malleable. He slept every day in the mote-dancing room with her belly curled into his. On his left hand he wore a long leather work glove. He stroked her fur, careful not to press down too hard, but risked being quilled. All these years, his hands had never traced the down on a woman's cheek or played in the thicket between her legs. Instead, he had touched only the cold spheres of glass eyes, the brittle scales on the legs of avian casualties, the pelts of trophy kills.

⟶

It was still summer. Day length was two hours shorter than in mid-July, but plenty long at fifteen hours, which the trees already knew.

Ghosts on Pale Stalks

Rain raps on the skylights, like tiny people trying to get in. This morning she thought she heard the whooshing of a burst water pipe, or was it the static of an untuned radio? Probably tinnitus, given her age. Old.

The whole point of being in this cabin was to chill out, tap into that deep well of whatever-it-was when you meditated, which she didn't. But the isolation had the opposite effect. It magnified every pain in her body and every irrational middle-aged emotion she was trying not to feel. Every time she tried to read her Oprah inspirational book (given to her by her well-meaning friend Joyce), she fell asleep. Not just asleep, but jaw-dropping-mouth-gaping-open asleep. Maybe this was the key. Like Sleeping Beauty, all she needed to do was to fall asleep for a few years, pass through this phase of her life and awake refreshed, no prince required. Except she would have a major kink in her back, a mustache, and her fingernails would be trailing on the ground.

She gave up on Oprah and rifled through the bookcase. In the games section there was a tiny deck of tarot cards, so small she could barely hold them in her adult hands. And she certainly could not read the accompanying teensy-weensy booklet without putting on her reading glasses, which she admitted to no one she needed. It occurred to her that maybe her life was out of focus because she couldn't actually *see*. She shuffled the cards and laid them out in a horseshoe pattern that seemed somewhat logical. Sometimes there was a glimmer of something if you gave yourself to the cards' wisdom. Of course, no one ever did tarot readings when they were *happy*.

It came out all swords. Swords stuck in stone walls, swords thrust into the ground, swords in a rat, swords impaling a deep red heart. *Well, that accurately sums up the situation.* She was a woman riddled with issues.

Just before she left for the island, she and her girlfriends had all joked about being crones.

"Remember, girls, that granny panties can also be worn on your head while housekeeping."

"Clean ones."

"And, ladies, after age fifty, never, ever, go anywhere without your tweezers."

They'd laughed so hard their receding gums showed. But she'd felt deeply that she really was a crone—frumpy, bitchy and wary (the three *other* dwarves)—a woman half straddling some other world. Someone with baggage. Over cocktails (dark and stormy, of course), Joyce had announced with her drink aloft, "From now on we vow to be done with anything that sucks our energy dry." They'd all clanked glasses. She knew what they were thinking when they'd looked at her. The urn.

At the cabin, it sits on the coffee table. Her relationship to the urn is problematic. Over the years it has acquired the power of an inverse magic genie lamp. Just looking at it makes her sad, yet she can't seem to part with it. She takes it everywhere with her. She can hear Joyce's words: "Oh for god's sake, Miriam, you need to get over that urn. You'll be dragging it to hell and back when you die."

She named them but never told anyone. She was not aware of the prohibition on cremation. When she met with a rabbi and learned that she had contravened burial laws, she wept for days afterward, believing she had defiled her babies and caused their souls harm. But over time, a different feeling took hold. She preferred having them near her where she could talk to them in private. When she moved, they came with her. They were always present in her life. Her parents did not approve, but then they also never forgave her for later marrying a Gentile and failing to expand the Siegel clan. *Fuck them.*

But maybe it *is* time to let go. She pours herself another nightcap.

The mouse in the bedroom ceiling chews all night. How a thing so small could sound like it is gnawing down an entire house is alarming. At three in the morning a freighter passes by, engines throbbing through the floorboards. She gets up and pours herself another drink, downing it in the kitchen. Finally she achieves something better than sleep—*blotto*, they used to call it.

In the morning, she packs the urn inside her jacket and heads to the ocean. It's raining and cool.

The tide is up, so there's no beach to walk on. She steps over the sea's afterbirth—tangles of bull kelp ribbons, slippery sea lettuce and rockweed—to walk along the logs strewn at the high tide mark. Her ex had practised how to throw his mother's remains from the plane by tossing flour on a trial run. He wanted to make it look dignified when he did it for real. Throwing ashes over Berlin, no less, which was illegal, but he did it anyway. Maybe she should have done a dry run. But no, she doesn't practise anything anymore. That is her practice. Rain starts coming down, sharply from an angle. Branches of a stunted apple tree poke into her face. She pushes them aside. At her feet is the tree's final harvest: a pool of round, undersized, lemon-yellow apples, like the suns that children draw.

A man with Brillo-pad hair springs out of a trailhead. He's wearing lime green boots. It is likely that he meditates. Maybe she should buy herself some lime green boots. His wet sheepdog gallops toward her and launches at her legs. Her balance falters—she teeters on the log dangerously and has to jump down. The urn falls out of her jacket but nothing spills. The man calls off his dog. "Hamish. Hamish!" When he reaches her, he smiles gently and is about to say something when he sees the urn in her hand. He hesitates. "Namaste," he clasps his palms together. "Be careful. It's windy out there." She nods, tucks the urn back inside her jacket, and steps back on the log, waving one arm out for balance. The rain tastes like the sea, metallic and kelpy.

On the bluff in the slanting rain, she feels a sudden apprehension. The wind yanks at her hood. Gloves off, she pulls out the urn from her jacket, which is now sopping wet. Water *resistant*. She removes the lid, stretches her arm out to the sea, turning her head away—as if one part of her is doing it but the other can't watch—and tilts the urn. It doesn't work. A gust comes up and blows remains back into her face and mouth: the ashes of her stillborns. This was not at all as cathartic as she had imagined. She should have practised. She retracts her arm, jams the lid back on the urn, leans into the rain and heads back to the cabin, her coat flapping wildly. *Some of them were lost to the wind.*

The woods behind the cabin seem like a better place to disperse the ashes. Dense cedar and salal, the old-growth forest, feel instantly calming. Arthritic maples creak; there are endless swathes of swordferns. Tiny birds twitter high up in the canopy. Were fairy tales of witches really just a distorted vision of middle-aged women and their particular sorrows? Her hands grip the urn's lid ever tighter. She won't let go. The cedars breathe, up and down, up and down, with their melancholy branches. She's always felt cedars were female.

She sits down on a mossy stump, not caring about getting wet, and listens to the rain. A soothing, intermittent rhythm. The urn beside her, nestled into the moss. At her feet is a clump of orange mushrooms a few inches high. They look like small, elongated ghosts, delicate and translucent, balancing on thin white stalks. They have raindrops on their oval heads. Water *resistant*. They lean toward her with their blank faces. She leans toward them. *Namaste*. The nurses didn't want her to see the babies. She screamed until they brought them. Two girls. Rose and Pearl. She'd said their names out loud.

⌐

Back at the cabin, the urn resumes its position on the coffee table. She finds an ancient pack of Craven menthol cigarettes on top of the fridge, sits on the couch and smokes one, popping out smoke rings. She starts telling the twins a story about a witch in the woods who adopts two children. There is someone at the door. The Brillo-haired man.

"Hello. I think these are yours." He hands over her gloves.

She thanks him. "Would you mind telling me where you got those lime green boots?"

So Sorry for Your Loss

From the killing jar, she'd inspected her specimen: *Acherontia styx*, the death's-head hawk moth. It could mimic the scent of bees and move undetected within a hive, talents she admired. She'd removed the moth from the jar with tweezers and laid it out on the spreading board. With her thumb and index finger, she'd gently squeezed the moth's thorax to make its wings spread, picked up the insect pin and guided it into the body. Next, she'd pinned the forewings. Then the hindwings. She'd placed the moth dorsal side up and drew her acrylics paint tray and brushes nearby. This was the moment she closed her eyes to contemplate the beauty in the death of all living things. The stillness. The form that is left behind. Cells that collapse, but pigments that remain. Insects could remain beautifully preserved for decades. Humans brought ugliness to death. She had seen Laurent Schwartz's hawk moth specimen at the Muséum de Toulouse last year and almost fainted. It had been her inspiration to go to Southeast Asia.

Medieval Yellow for the hindwings. Cadmium Yellow where the hind wings met the frenulum. The blue horizontal lines on the abdomen: Royal Blue, Silver. It had taken three paint sessions to capture the nuances of the scales. But the Styx family had been pleased with this wifely tribute to their patriarch. "So sorry for your loss," she had said after practising the phrase out loud at home. It never came naturally.

⟶

As she spoke about the hornet moth and its masterful mimicking of a hornet in flight, her psychiatrist examined dirt under his fingernails. It had been a tradition in her family, collecting and preserving. Whole rooms in their house were devoted to artefacts of some runaway obsession: embroidered silk gloves from the Victorian era, dried reptiles rescued from a museum in Cairo, row upon row of colonial bob wigs from early America, hand and leg prostheses designed by sixteenth-century French military doctor Ambroise Paré, a rare copperplate engraving of *Duroia eriopila* from *Metamorphosis insectorum Surinamensium* by seventeenth-century naturalist Maria Sibylla Merian, shrunken heads from Ecuador, and common prayer books containing profane doodles and marginalia confiscated by the Episcopalian authorities. In this respect, moths were hardly eccentric. But of course, she had not yet revealed what she actually did with the moths. And the people who shared their names.

"Well, I hope, Madame Styx, we will be able to resolve or at least alleviate your anxiety about this, er... collecting obsession." He held the door open for her, as her honey-ish body odour enveloped him.

Mme. Styx gathered her cape from the coat rack, slipped on her silk gloves and returned home to her rented studio on Rue Coteau (or Chu Vănan An Street, as she did not like to call it). She enjoyed being called Mme. Styx. It had a dark, mythical air to it. She realized that the situation had escalated, especially after her fifth and most recent marriage to the stockbroker. Mr. Styx, or rather the former Mr. Styx. Black market Lepidoptera were getting difficult to find. *Attacus atlas* specimens were still not available. Climate change had decimated some of the rarest species. The authorities might have their suspicions about her, but she felt compelled to continue. Being on the back side of the building was convenient—darker and less conspicuous. Of course, lots of other residents in the not-so-upscale quarter also hung out their laundry to dry. But hers was not really laundry. And she left it hanging all night.

She pegged the weighted bed sheet to the short line, switched on the black light and stepped back to admire the ultraviolet glow. The collecting jars were at the ready. A few hours later the luminous sheet would be a canvas decorated with the bodies of light-seeking Lepidoptera. One in particular captured her interest: *Bombyx mori*. The silk moth.

⟶

She continued her daily visits to Dr. Mori. She didn't really need the psychiatrist. Well, yes she did, but not as a psychiatrist. As a man with a name she cherished: Mori. Their connection developed slowly, just as she had planned. She noticed he was susceptible to the perfume she had engineered and continued to wear it. Marriage would come soon enough.

⟶

Madame Styx, now Madame Mori, a.k.a. Delores Wolff, stepped into her studio, closed the door and removed her gloves. She had already disposed of the smothering cloth. She stood silently on the mat. Night was the best time of day. She usually felt calm after dispatching her human specimen, but tonight she was anxious. She poured herself a double Manhattan.

She held the killing jar up to the glare from the porch light. Thanks to the sodium cyanide crystals, *Bombyx mori* had succumbed. With watchmaker's tweezers, she lifted it out by the thorax and placed it on a black cloth on the work table, admiring the creamy colour of the moth's body, the myriad individual scales on its wings, its feathery antennae, so adept at sensing sexual pheromones. Painting it would be an exacting exercise in capturing gradations of white. A specimen so simple and beautiful it almost made her cry.

She got up to wash and dry her hands. On the way back to the table she caught a glance of herself in the hallway mirror. Wrinkles were starting around her mouth. A vague image from earlier flashed across her mind. There was a mirror in her husband's office which, if you stood in a certain position in the room, meant that you could be seen from the apartment across the alley.

She had made a mistake. This would be her last. It was unfortunate her collection would be incomplete.

Walk on Water

Several questions had occurred to Saul as he drove away from his first "self-branding" workshop. For instance, what were the possibilities of becoming a sculptor after twenty years as a business analyst? Could you actually become aroused by the sight of a woman's—what was that word—*décolletage*? And what was that line the career coach had said about "becoming impeccable to yourself"? He noticed the tic in the coach's left eyelid when he said that phrase. Maybe the guy just made that stuff up based on what happened to him the night before. Saul was more interested in the story behind the tic than all the hoo-hah about marketing or branding yourself which, frankly, made him picture sad, naked, unemployed people in their dirty kitchens brandishing a hot iron to their backsides. He didn't want to be a "brand" of himself. What he really wanted was to *be himself*, and he had woefully lost track of what that was.

The coach, Wayne, had warned the class of executive clients, a.k.a. terminated people, not to take an emotional stance on their joblessness that was out of proportion to their actual situation. "This is an opportunity," he chimed over and over. Opportunity to reassess your goals. Opportunity to hone your CV. Opportunity to match your Myers-Briggs personality type (ENTP: extroverted-intuitive-thinking-perceiving) to your ideal job. *Opportunity to drink during the day*, Saul had added, to himself. Half the class hadn't done their resumé homework and were scolded. Saul was one of them. He knew already that his professional CV, his LinkedIn account, his "unique selling point," were now historical artefacts, utterly useless. He was shedding himself. So, instead of making sure the top of his resumé hit all the self-branding buttons within thirty seconds, he'd spent thirty minutes on YouTube watching Werner Herzog's *Cave of Forgotten Dreams*, marvelling at the litheness of wild cattle painted thirty thousand years ago. It put his current situation in perspective.

He wasn't sure where he was driving to, but it wasn't to go home to Madeline. So he pointed the car toward Richmond, not West Vancouver. Being "terminated"—he hated "let go," it sounded too much like releasing a balloon—was strange. It made him feel eviscerated, no him anymore, just an empty hide, shaky lines on a cave wall. In the kitchen on the day of his termination, Madeline glaring at him with her hard-set mouth, he had blurted out, "Your lips are not where I want them to be." What the hell did he mean? He wished he could ask Zaya out: that woman from Macchiato. Maybe if he was ten years younger, employed and single. She had a face like an Egyptian goddess, only she was Iranian. And the most exquisite clavicles, when visible. She could give him a tic any time. But more seriously, deep inside her eyes he saw *potential*. If he became small enough to slip down through the black pupils of her eyes, where might he find himself?

She has a waist like the curve of a jaguar's back, he thought and immediately saw the elegant charcoal hide of the paleolithic elk at Lascaux. "Become impeccable, become impeccable," he repeated out loud, whizzing along Bridgeport Road. The car emitted a wail like the sound of a dog chained to a post. *Downshift! Jesus Christ, this bloody Flintstones car*. The traffic slowed. Despite the challenges of driving his son's Chevy Cavalier, called in inner circles "the shitbox," he took a perverse pleasure in sitting behind the wheel in a three-hundred-dollar

Armani dress shirt, grinding the gears of an engine hovering on the cusp of catastrophe. Courting incongruity was his new raison d'être.

A traffic jam clogged the overpass. Signs along Bridgeport advertised an "Asian Night Market." Up ahead, cars were bumper to bumper, negotiating a slow, snaking, jerking line leading to a massive parking lot in a former industrial zone. He had a hankering to plunge into a mass of people and feed on that energy of random, rambling, goal-less pleasure. Yes, that was his new goal: goal-lessness. To be *peccable* to himself. Peccable. He liked the chickeny sound of it.

He handed his parking fee to the long-fingernailed woman in the cubicle, parked, and entered the fray. Asians and non-Asians alike jostled shoulder to shoulder, sucking up liquids with small brown balls in the bottom and extracting wormy noodles from takeout boxes. Screams from the fairway ride thrill-seekers arched over the crowds. Past the stalls of Hello Kitty socks and cutesy cellphone covers was a section devoted to the usual fairway games—shoot the duck, toss the hoop over the bottle—with the usual hideous prizes that would moulder in some child's bedroom for years to come. But he had no taste for anything that required aiming at a target.

A sign caught his eye. "Walk on Water: Take the Bubble Challenge!" There was a rectangular above-ground pool and people inside large plastic bubbles were wobbling across the water's surface, mostly with spectacular unsuccess. What a weird thing to do. He stood watching as they slipped backwards, crawled on hands and knees or just plain flailed inside their wonky planets while "Rolling on the River" blasted over a loudspeaker. People trapped inside their own neurotically outsized thought bubbles, like the two child-free people he and his wife now were since the kids flew the coop.

He had a sudden impulse to do it.

One emphatic push and he rolled out into the pool: mild terror, a distorted view, limbs in the wrong places. The trick was not to apply earthbound movements to an essentially unstable platform.

Crawling? Possibly. Floundering, counterproductive, even injurious. Non-terrestrial walking? Yes. He had to imagine himself to be a cross between a human perpetual motion machine and a crazed hamster inside a paddle wheel. For the scheduled ten minutes, he did just that.

When he scrambled out of the bubble, his land legs balked. There it was: the deadening trick of gravity. Everything reduced again to the vertical and the horizontal. Bipedal boringness. Still unstable on his feet, he relearned walking, aimed for the food stalls, past people eating spiral potato chips on skewers that looked like the spine of some prehistoric animal. He ate an entire plate of deep-fried chicken knees, biting down on the cartilage as if breaking down the structure of his own body.

⌒

Saul had a good severance package from his former employer, so right now money was not an issue. He had time to explore his next move. But what an idiot he was, thinking he could just chisel a few chunks off a slab of stone and call himself a sculptor. He didn't know the first thing about sculpture, except he liked the man crawling out of a clamshell at the Museum of Anthropology. He wasn't even sure how the hell he came up with the idea. But once it stuck, he spent hours at his computer watching YouTube and Vimeo, documentaries of sculptors at work, hanging on their every word. Antony Gormley was genius. Madeline hovered, impatient with his status. Any time she glimpsed the images on his computer screen she huffed, snorting air out her nostrils. She had become a woman of few words since the kids had moved out.

He signed up for a sculpting class for non-artists at Langara College, joining the ranks of the artistically ungifted, the unconfident and the overconfident. His cohorts were a shy Japanese woman named Etsuko, a nose-pierced, angry young woman who seemed perennially electrified, a very nice middle-aged woman, Marjorie, whose exclamation of choice was "Oh, heavens," and a slim thirty-year-old guy who had the presence of a tree, in a good way. Llewellyn, their instructor, was an aficionado of the human figure and happened to be a fan of the aforementioned Antony Gormley, too.

"If you consider his collection of body casts, you can see that he's really exploring how it feels to inhabit your body, publicly and privately," he said, leaning on one arm against the oak desk as if he were Gene Kelly with his jaunty cane. "What space does it occupy? Who can or can't enter your Personal Zone?" He hovered close to Etsuko, who leaned away from him. The class shifted in their desks. Behind the instructor loomed a slide of the sculpture *Execution of Duty*, a tenfold repetition of the same upright naked man, holding a briefcase, which Saul found depressing.

"Your final exercise in this course, which we will be leading up to with smaller assignments, will be to create a sculptural impression of your own body, to convey the shape, the tone and posture that reveal some aspect of who you are. Try to choose a pose that has meaning to you but that's comfortable to hold. Or even better, let your creator choose the pose." They all walked out of the classroom slightly hunched.

Saul had been excited about the class until he heard what the final assignment was. A life cast meant having someone slather him in Vaseline and plaster gauze and then him standing like an idiot till he dried. He briefly considered quitting or taking up the saxophone, but the idea of doing something tactile seemed better than staring down data-flow diagrams or business requirement documents.

He kept driving his son's shitty car even after the part for his Audi came in. It gave him a spirit of raw youth, new beginnings. He gave up on the branding seminars but kept on with career coaching. When he mentioned the Bubble Challenge to his coach Wayne, that familiar left eye twitched for a second, then his coach burst out in a huge grin and asked, "Can I use that in the 'Change Is Your Best Friend' workshop?" But when Saul brought up the sculptor idea, Wayne wasn't quite as enthusiastic. He sat staring at Saul with his lips pursed, tapping his index finger on Saul's file.

"But Wayne, I'm an ENTP trapped in a corporate wonk's body," Saul protested.

The Macchiato became a regular thing. Zaya was always on mornings. When he arrived he took care not to sit near the "dog lady," a dour old woman with a small shuddering brown poodle that suffered constant reprimands from its mistress: "Felix! Sit down! Felix, be quiet!" Saul sat as far as possible from dog lady to avoid hearing her harangues and having to watch the poor dog shrink in submission. The only person in the café who was kind to that woman was Zaya.

Saul would order his usual and engage in a kind of chaste wooing with Zaya. No, not a wooing. A courting. Flirting? Flourting. He found her demureness refreshing in an age of in-your-face plastic beauty. No drawn-on eyebrows or fake eyelashes like the rest of the young set these days, including his dangerously beautiful daughter, who had absconded to Toronto. Zaya didn't compete with anyone. She radiated peace and a deep compassion. Even though she worked in a lowly coffee shop he thought of her as noble.

"Good morning, Saul!" she called to him as he ordered. "Latte is on its way."

Not surprisingly, Zaya, who struck him as being smarter than she let on, had already progressed from cashier to barista and had started decorating his coffees with this and that, a leaf, a spiral, cocoa swirls that he swore looked like Arabic script. He knew all the baristas did that for customers, but still.

"Grande latte double shot, Saaaaul..." she almost sang his name with an uprise in her voice that hung tenderly in the air. They exchanged quiet smiles as he approached the counter and picked up the cup. Their eyes met. Today there was a heart outlined on top, a very distinct heart. It felt like sacrilege to take a sip and ruin it. He thought this might be the right time to ask her about modelling for his life-drawing assignment.

"Zaya. I have a question," he said, clutching his cup. She nodded. "I'm taking a sculpture class, and we have an assignment to draw a bust. Would you be interested?"

"Bust?" She looked startled.

"No, not bust-bust, just the head," he answered stupidly. "I need to sketch you, then—"

Her face flushed. She looked down. "Oh no, I don't think so. Thank you." She turned away from him and scurried into the back. *Idiot.*

Gradually Saul took to the at-loose-ends lifestyle and shed much of his corporate Teflon, becoming less arrogant, more casual, more himself. A self, not a "sellable point." The pre-kids Saul. Or maybe the post-kids Saul. His dress shirts moved further back in the closet. But Zaya seemed to move in the opposite direction. Her blouses became more conservative, her figure obscured by their frumpy shapes, a reverse metamorphosis. One day she was wearing a head scarf. She avoided eye contact. He couldn't bear to look at the scarf. It wasn't even one of the pretty ones that some immigrant women allowed themselves. It filled him with sadness. He thought it was his fault, asking if she would model for him. Venturing that far beyond their coffee context had pushed them into the awkward zone.

The hearts on his lattes disappeared. He maintained a polite relation with her, wondering how he could smooth things between them.

One day *she* disappeared. He hoped that she had taken advantage of one of those employee education perks to advance beyond being a barista.

As long as he had severance wages, he kept up his slack approach to re-employment, which included going back to the Night Market and the Bubble Challenge stall. Mostly to watch. It was fascinating, the different looks on people's faces: hilarity, fear, frustration, entrapment, confusion, delight, determination. A carnival glimpse into the human psyche. Some of them came out of the balls laughing, others with the rounded eyes of the terrorized. Madeline had made efforts to repair things on the home front, although he was resisting them. The air felt thick and impenetrable when the two of them were together. Eventually, she twigged that something was up.

"So, you go to this 'branding' seminar, but you come home smelling like a barbecue. Why is that?"

"Because I'm not at the seminar."

"Right."

"I go to Walk on Water."

"Oh, for Christ's sake, Saul, stop the bullshit."

"No, really, it's called 'Walk on Water.' It's this huge bubble you roll around in at the Asian Night Market."

"You go to the Asian Night Market? With whom?"

"No one. Me. You can come if you want."

⌐

He watched Madeline get zipped into the ball. She looked game. She looked like a Nordic huntress trapped in a snow globe, ready to traverse the icy waters of the North Sea. Saul suddenly realized he could never picture Zaya doing something like this.

The attendant zipped up his bubble and rolled him into the pool and smack into Madeline. *Sneaky bastard.* She tried to scrabble away, but Saul gave chase—as much as you can, flip-flopping like a sock in a dryer. Madeline, always the strategist, turned course 180 degrees and dog-walked into him, the collision having on him the desired clown-slips-on-banana-peel effect. She stuck her tongue out at him mockingly. Their eyes met through the plastic spheres. The blue waters sloshed against their bubbles. An adolescent boy passed by, water walking, legs apart like a striding giant. It was as though they were all fantastical creatures fighting for space in a cluttered pond. Madeline shouted something to him through the ball, but it sounded like underwater snorkel talk. He gestured back in his bubble sign language, and she seemed to understand. They both made the "X-I'm done" sign to the attendant at the same time. Madeline rolled out of the pool ahead of him.

As he extracted himself from the bubble, he looked up at his wife waiting for him with her disheveled silver hair, hands on her ample hips, her too-small mouth in a broad smile. Yes, a Nordic goddess who could strangle a man with her bare hands. Or smear him in bear grease. Or Vaseline.

Three days later he saw Zaya. She was in the mall on a Monday morning, walking with a bag of groceries in each hand, behind a frowning man who looked twenty years her senior. She wore a huge baggy gown that hung like a slack sail over her body. Between her and the man in front of her was a deliberate and irrevocable space. Saul didn't speak to her.

⟜

Once the gauze plaster had dried, Madeline started to remove the front body cast from Saul's torso by pulling gently.

"Feeling a bit hollowed out, hon," he laughed, but had to stop for fear of ruining the mold.

"We can laugh when you're down to just the Vaseline layer," she said, placing his plaster chest gently on the table.

Dried Fish Woman,
Herbivore Man

He is Shinya. But he prefers Shane. He looks like a boy trapped in a man's body—pale, freckled skin, and a grin. Short cowboy legs. And his tie's too short. Doesn't look thirty-two. The woman across from him is Mitsuko. He's distracted by her eyebrows: painted-on black strips that look like skid marks.

Mitsuko is a lab technician at Tokyo Tech who follows a peculiar diet with prohibitions on coffee, alcohol, sugar, wheat and fat—everything Shinya subsists on, the evidence strewn around his apartment: empty takeout boxes, *makudonarudo* burger wrappers, disposable coffee cups, and *kentakkii* fried chicken buckets, their various funks carousing together into one universal food pong. He's thinking he should have taken her to Akitaya restaurant, near Hamamatsucho Station. They could have had grilled organ meat and cheap beer, except she says she doesn't drink.

They met on the *kuwagata* forum for staghorn beetle collectors. Although they're not really collectors. They've already exchanged beetle photos. Shinya had originally coveted an *o-kuwagata*, the largest, most expensive staghorn beetle, but instead bought the cheaper *kuwagata* and spent money on his "girlfriend," Kyoko. When Mitsuko first saw his beetle photo, she'd texted back, "Shinya, your beetle's not male. It is female. Look at the antennae—shorter." He thought he'd bought a juvenile male. It's true he's had little experience with females. When he'd tried to impress Mitsuko with his red special-edition KFC phone from China—Huawei android, 5.5-inch 720p display, 12MP camera—she'd said, "Whaaa?"

Other than their pet beetles, they don't have much in common. Shane finds Mitsuko a little too plain and small-busted since he's gotten used to Kyoko's perfect features. That being said, he's a little plain himself. He drives a produce truck. His family had been small-scale farmers in Kurume, but he'd left the familial slave labour for a better life in the city. When he misses the orchards, he helps Kyoko place oranges or peaches in a large crystal bowl on the counter so their fragrance fills the apartment. She understands his needs.

Mitsuko has posters of Audrey Hepburn all over her apartment. She imagines herself to be like the famous waif, but the gap between her aspiration and the reality is much larger than she assumes, plus she does not sport a cigarette holder. Hepburn is a doe stepping through a field of flowers; Mitsuko is a dormouse hiding under a toadstool. For ten years she has practised the Audrey smile, and various other smiles, in the mirror, trying to find the one that should inhabit her face. All have failed her.

Now, with Shinya across from her, he models the kind of smile that has eluded her since the age of thirty.

He is good-natured, Mitsuko thinks, if somewhat ignorant, and hardly embarrassed about his lingering bumpkin origins. And yet, there is some rudimentary energy in operation underneath these shortfalls. He makes her laugh. When he talks, his arms and hands shoot in all directions like fireworks.

"My *kuwagata*'s name is Renaado. Leonard," she says. She believes Renaado has a soul. A Buddhist, not a Christian soul.

"Leonard?"

"Because he is dark and mysterious like the singer, Leonard Cohen. Who was also a Buddhist."

"Ah," Shinya answers, pretending to know who Leonard Cohen is, and embarrassed that he had not named his beetle.

"What's yours called?"

"Uh. Rabbit. Like Bugs Bunny."

She'd bought Renaado from the famous *kuwagata* store Mushi-sha in Nakano. He had bought his from a vending machine. He wasn't that particular.

⌐

They meet again, the third time, at Bar Araku. He's convinced her to try a sake mojito. Now he's urging her to try the kangaroo burgers, but she's fiddling with a playlist on her phone and shows him the screen.

"Do you know this song? Su-zaaanne.... It is the poet from Canada." Mitsuko is passionate about Leonard Cohen. She knows all his song lyrics in English.

"I like Justin Timberlake. Ooohhhh..." Shinya sings, miming a microphone. "But Canada. I would not want to go there!"

"Why not?"

"Too cold. And the women wear glasses and drive buses." Shinya wipes his greasy hands on his jeans.

Mitsuko looks down and squares her placemat with the edge of the table. She had worn her contacts today. There are times when Shinya's ignorant answers aren't worth addressing. But part of his allure is his lack of decorum. He never puts on airs or pretends he's someone else. Status doesn't concern him the way it obsesses her family. Her parents live and will die obsessed with how others judge their worthiness.

But with Shinya she can be herself. She can figure out, even, who "herself" could be. He's incapable of intrigue. Being in his presence makes her conscious of all the gestures and postures she assumes in public that are encrustations of snobbery: crossing her legs, tilting her head, fixing her gaze on him adoringly when he speaks but not really hearing what he's saying. These actions are all insincere. And he's immune to them.

"I just like it, having the beetle there. It's like company while you're watching TV. But I hate the bug poetry." Shinya opens his jaws on the kangaroo burger.

Mitsuko is amazed at how big his mouth is. She tells him she feels embarrassed to go into the pet store to buy supplies. She orders online. Or if she has to go in person, she says it's a gift for her *kuwagata*-crazy nephew.

⌒

They've known each other for five months now. It's really about the beetles, they tell themselves, after another dinner out, or after another excursion to Tama's Insectarium, or a whisky sampling at Asyl now that Mitsuko's drinking alcohol.

Behind their backs, people call them *Himono onna* and *Shoshoku*—Dried Fish Woman and the Herbivore Man. But Mitsuko doesn't consider herself a sexless spinster. She's an independent woman uninterested in the trappings of motherhood or wifehood. Yes, she had rented a fake boyfriend a couple of times, once for an office party and once to placate her parents at a large family gathering, but other than that she considers herself happily single. And as for Shinya, it would never occur to him that he's *Shoshoku*—uninterested in sex—or that he's forsworn love and intimacy. He has Kyoko whenever he wants, romantic encounters that he designs himself and enjoys thoroughly, and intimacy that's clean and unencumbered, with a female who has every feature of beauty (down to the oval-shaped birthmark on her right thigh) that makes loving her easy.

Shinya has a telescope fixed on the apartment building across the street. The telescope is for Kyoko, catering to her fashion obsession. He helps her get positioned in front of it so she can spy what the women are wearing when they leave the building for work or pleasure. Sometimes when Shinya comes home from work she's still leaning there with her face pressed against the eyepiece. He has to make her stand up and stop gazing because it makes a circular indent under her eye. Before he met Mitsuko the sight of the telescope on the window ledge made him feel empty, like someone he once loved from afar had disappeared from his life.

He sits at the table with Kyoko, or OK as he calls her sometimes, smiling into her green eyes. As always, his *karee raisu* (curry rice) is in his favourite bowl, centred on the placemat. On the counter, Rabbit, his now-named staghorn beetle, stands sentry on her oak twig. She looks artificial half the time, posed, but at night she forages around in her beetle matting, making lots of noise. Shinya keeps Rabbit's habitat meticulously clean, misting the dirt regularly and replacing used jelly dishes. The beetle zone is much tidier than the Shinya zone. One day, Shinya will have to tell Mitsu about Kyoko.

At Christmas (while their beetles are hibernating), they preorder a KFC party barrel. *Kurisumasu ni wa kentakkii.* Kentucky chicken for Christmas. Japanese tradition! They buy each other gifts. From Mitsuko to Shinya: a *kuwugata* T-shirt that says: *Beetles are better than People.* From Shinya to Mitsuko: a beautifully crafted wooden specimen box from Shiga Konchu Kukyu-sha. Shinya holds up his T-shirt.

"Oh no, they gave me the wrong size. It's too small," Mitsuko says.

"But it's perfect for *you*, Mitsu. Put it on. You don't realize that you actually bought this shirt for yourself." She slips it over her head. She never wears T-shirts, but it looks good. Shinya snaps a photo and sends it to her on Snapchat. She hands the specimen box back over to Shinya. He pauses.

"I used to go to the park with my father to catch beetles. I had the nets, everything. There were lots of beetles back then. Much easier to find than now. My father promised to make me a specimen box years ago. But he died before that was possible."

In the spring they go to a movie. Something cowboy. *Sukiyaki Western Django*. Mitsuko feels like her eyeballs have been peeled and removed. Swords. Machine guns. Pillaging. Murder. So many things blowing up. At the end, Shinya puts his arm around her for the first time.

"May I formally ask? Rabbit would like to marry Renaado. I know it's backwards, but they're beetles." Mitsuko could smell the faint musk of his armpit near her shoulder. It was not as romantic a proposal as she would have liked. But she says yes.

They consider having a beetle-loving priest marry the bugs. Instead they take the train to Kamakura, and at the foot of its famous Great Buddha, pledge their acceptance of the arranged marriage.

Araku's air conditioners are going full blast. Outside, pedestrians pass in a stream of steaming wet umbrellas.

"I was thinking, Mitsu…." The straw from Mitsuko's cocktail is inserted between her pursed lips as she listens. "Shouldn't our beetles live together? Now that they're married. They'll only live a few more years." Shinya waits with his nail-bitten fingers poised on the table. A long stream of crushed mint and sake courses up Mitsuko's straw.

"Yes, Shane. I think so."

A year and a half ago she'd put her name on the list for a 2-LDK apartment (living/dining/kitchen) in Shibuya, thinking that when her aging parents needed care they could all live together there. The agency called Thursday and said one is now available. She isn't so keen about living with her parents anymore. She has a different idea. Shinya likes it. Cohabitation.

She worries that they might be asked for a marriage certificate, but when they meet with the agent no questions are asked. Maybe it's their age. They sign the agency papers. Oddly, such freedom from scrutiny makes them feel as if they've gotten away with an indiscretion, as if they really were a modern, uncommitted couple.

That night, Shinya puts Kyoko back in her box. He feels her size D breasts one last time. He had named her after Kyoko Fukada, the famous Japanese actress. Another one of his hopeless obsessions. She'd never written him back. His Kyoko is only 157 centimetres tall. She weighs twenty-five kilograms. Sexual tri-function, mouth thirteen centimetres deep. He preferred the blonde wig. He bends her knees so she can curl up in the box. It was worth paying for the moveable joints.

⁓

Mitsuko and Shinya stand next to each other on the tatami mats in the apartment. The two old beetle cases are at their feet, empty. There is a new case there, a longer, larger one with a partition in the middle. Renaado is on one side, Rabbit on the other. There is fresh bedding. Mitsuko feels as if her heart is, not breaking, but that the folded-in corners are lifting. Beside her thigh, Shinya's right index fingertip flutters up imperceptibly, the way someone in deep sleep might twitch when the wind moves the curtains.

Ripiddu Nivicatu

"What the hell was that?" Deep grunts came from the dark shrubbery beyond the villa's patio. Celine moved her chair away from the sound. Her husband, Jean-Paul, moved toward it, his huge hands raised to hush everyone.

"Wild boar."

He'd taken up hunting last year and had already become a self-described expert. At home his freezer was full of whole wild hares, venison haunches and various mammal parts. Their front door knocker was a cast-iron buffalo head.

"There's two sounds a wild boar'll make. One when he knows you're there and one when he doesn't. This one knows we're here." He inched closer to the edge of the property. No one could see his eyes—the fanaticism—as he stared out at where the Tyrrhenian Sea would be. Something boar-sized scrambled in a panic down the bank.

"The Sicilian ones here are really black swine," he said, returning to the patio. "But they're still classed with *sus scrofa scrofa* like the ones I shot in Czech Republic last year." Not everyone was as fascinated as he was with porcine taxonomy.

Celine tuned him out. She thought back to the morning. They had just got back from swimming in the sea—she paddled, he did his competition strokes—and her skin was still salty and sticky. She felt alive. Jean-Paul had leaned in to kiss her but she had turned away. It's difficult to love a man who has a schedule even for sex.

"If a boar doesn't know you're there, it's a softer huffing: hmph, hmmmphh," Jean-Paul explained to Alexander, his natural father, and Evelyn, his father's—whatever she was.

He could be captivating when he was the centre of attention, but as soon as he talked hunting he lost his ability to gauge his audience. He became a know-it-all. Before dinner he'd asked Celine to gut the sea bream he'd bought from the Cefalù market. To his specifications. She had refused. She couldn't stomach the gelled eyes of a dead fish. Paulo volunteered, in her defence, despite his own squeamishness. She overheard them in the kitchen. "No, no, cut behind the gills, Paulo, behind. Take the head right off!" Even without looking, she could tell her son was struggling with the task. He was a sensitive soul. His lips quivered at the slightest provocation. Jean-Paul was angry that at eight years old Paulo still couldn't run a five-kilometre marathon. He thought Paulo lacked initiative.

Since it was pointless to intervene in the gutting lesson, she'd gone out to sweep the patio. At home she never swept. But at the villa it had become a meditation, an obsession to clear the debris. On holidays she felt inert. All this time to lie around and admit things to yourself. The things that drag you down, the unfinished things. That was as far as she had got in defining it. At the back of her mind she had a crazy idea to move here. Cultivate something. Although the soil looked unforgiving. The Sicilian they spoke to in the olive grove at Collesano had pointed at the stunted trees and said, "You have to grow them on the limit of what they can bear." She was not sure she liked the sound of that.

"Well, Jean-Paul, you've convinced me now it was a boar!" Evelyn laughed in the dark, causing one of the candles to flicker. They all tipped their heads back and observed the constellations. The intense heat of the afternoon lingered.

"That's Hercules up there," Jean-Paul observed incorrectly, "slaying the dragon. When I'm out hunting I sometimes feel like there's what we see, and then behind that, there's a *purer reality*. What animals see. We get little glimpses of it and then—it evaporates," Jean-Paul waved his hand dramatically, clearly pleased with his philosophical idea.

"There's no point believing in a *purer reality*, Jean-Paul. Our perception is all we have. Instead of believing there's something more ideal behind what we perceive, trust your *given* senses. Not some abstraction that may or may not be true." Nobody responded. Alexander's speech often had that effect on people. The velvet darkness poured down from above.

"Oh! There's a shooting star." Evelyn pointed, her many bracelets jingling. But in the usual fashion of celestial ephemera it vanished before anyone else could spot it. Celine wondered how old Evelyn was. Considerably younger than Jean-Paul's father.

Celine had agreed to come on this trip on one condition: separate beds. So far, this had worked well. Except for the two giant floodlights from the resort complex below, shining all night into the bedroom window like the reflective eyes of a nocturnal beast. And past the resort, a pump powered on and off, as if an iron lung were inflating and deflating. It made her vigilant in her sleep. It sounded like something wounded was labouring in the darkness. Jean-Paul never heard it. He was a heavy sleeper.

Paulo appeared on the patio in his ninja pajamas.

"Oh, is he sleepwalking?" Evelyn asked, her botoxed brow remaining in place.

The boy leaned into his mother's ear and whispered.

"Non, non, Pippo. It was only us moving the chairs." The boy shook his head.

"Non. Le lit a tremblé. I felt it."

"We didn't feel any trembling here, Pippo." Celine gave him a glass of water and steered him back to bed. He snuck back and spoke quietly to his mother. "He says he wants to say goodnight to Grandpapa Alex. *Vas-y.*" She nudged him forward.

"Goodnight, Paulo," Alex smiled, then did a comical salute to cheer the boy up. Paulo mimicked one back, then marched off to bed.

"He said he felt the bed shake. He often gets up in the night and wanders. He has very vivid dreams. Oh, Jean-Paul, remember sitting on the patio in Montpellier—was it Fête de Saint-Jean?—and Paulo came out—"

Jean-Paul leapt in. "He had his hands in front of him like a zombie. It was hilarious. He was walking in his sleep saying, 'Find the roebuck. Fiiiind the roebuck.'" He finished her story as he always did and sucked back his beer.

"Find the roebuck?" his father said.

"Earlier in the day I was teaching Paulo how to imitate a doe in heat. It calls in the roebuck."

"So you can kill it," Celine piped in.

Evelyn leaned in to Jean-Paul. "That sounds pretty advanced for a little guy."

"That's what *I* said, Evelyn. He hides in the bushes like a commando and uses this rubber squeezy thing to make sounds and fool them."

"It's called a roe deer call, Celine."

"It's cheating." Celine hated her husband's commitment to "compassionate killing."

"Well, anyway, first I use this softer call that mimics a fawn separated from its mother. This draws the doe away from the buck."

"So you can kill it."

"If that doesn't work, I ramp up the volume and do a doe call. That attracts a lone buck. It's an art. You have to understand animal behaviour."

"Ah, the art of romance in a rubber squeezy ball!" Evelyn chanted.

"Oh yes, and there's terror and jealousy calls, too. If you want to get really advanced, imitate the call of a doe in heat. Woo! Brings him in every time." He elbows Celine.

"The 'come hither' song!" Evelyn glanced over at Alexander.
Celine stood up suddenly. "I'm off to bed."

⁓

The moment Celine left, the rhythm of the group shifted. The stars became the silent focus of attention. Guard dogs barked from the empty villas in the hills. The pump station below heaved on and off, as if the landscape were struggling to breathe.

Jean-Paul restrained himself from asking his father why he'd deserted him and his mother and France so long ago and moved far away to Australia. It was five years ago that he'd first met Alex. He knew well enough now that there was no point discussing the past. His father lived only in the present. And his home was any port he could sail to. Jean-Paul thought back to the day his mother had taken him to buy new swim trunks after he'd passed his junior level swim lessons. He'd reached an age where he found it embarrassing to be in public with his mother, let alone buying swim trunks and having her view his developing anatomy. She was sitting on the bench in the change room while he stood there in his Speedo with his spidery thin legs. She was looking down at her gnarled toes in the hippie sandals she always wore. "You have a father, you know. He lives in New South Wales," she'd said. Their eyes met and the story of his life up to that moment collapsed.

"It takes a certain personality to be a hunter. I'm not sure I could do it," Evelyn tried to keep up the thread.

Alexander looked pointedly at his son. "I could do it. But I choose not to."

"But wasn't your father in some kind of regiment?" Jean-Paul asked.

"Yes. He even had a rifle."

"Do you know what kind?"

"Yes. The killing kind he used on himself."

⌒

Just before 4:00 a.m. a small tremor occurred, originating from Etna's southeast crater, a barely detectable ripple, like a tiny wave coming to shore. Only Paulo momentarily stirred.

⌒

In the morning while everyone slept in, the villa maintenance man came. Silently he ran his long-handled net over and over the pool's surface, gathering leaves and dead bees, then slipped away unnoticed. In the treetops, the sound of heat and listlessness began. The cicadettas had started early. Everyone ate breakfast together in the shade, then retreated to their respective abodes on the property. Jean-Paul stood alone on the patio and watched his father and Evelyn giggle their way up the path to the studio.

Celine and Jean-Paul had argued after breakfast. For their last night she wanted to make *ripiddu nivicatu* for dinner, especially for Paulo.

"Snow-covered volcanic ash?"

"He's crazy about volcanoes. It's Mount Etna made of rice blackened with cuttlefish ink, topped with ricotta for snow and tomatoes for the molten lava." It sounded childish to Jean-Paul and not very gourmet, so he'd vetoed it.

Celine came out onto the patio now, loaded with towels and beach paraphernalia. Jean-Paul saw the plastic shovel and bucket.

"Paulo, you're too old for making sandcastles," he said, roughing up his son's blonde hair. Paulo squirmed away from his father's hand and sidled up to his mother. Celine said nothing. They disappeared down the steep path to the public beach, leaving Jean-Paul stranded.

He retreated to the house to take his cold morning shower. As he stood under the shower head, he heard something. A wild animal? He craned his neck. Something moaning. Not a dog. He turned off the water and moved up against the shower wall to listen. They said there were red foxes up in the Madonie mountains. No. A wild boar in the daytime wasn't likely either. He waited for the sound again, opened the window a little. It was his father and Evelyn in the studio. Making love. Loudly. He couldn't believe it. In this heat. It was shocking how they went at it. He opened the window all the way and jammed his back against the wet tiles. Evelyn was keening intermittently now, the sound escalating up the scale. She called out ecstatically at climax. The lovemaking subsided, returning the morning to the high-voltage shrill of the native cicadettas.

Jean-Paul slumped down into the tub. Some long-acquired psychic armour gave way in his body. It occurred to him that, given he was born in February, this was how he was conceived—in a tender fit of passion on a hot summer day. No plan other than mutual pleasure, unscripted and carefree. A dalliance. His mother and father never married or saw each other again, whereas he had married Celine because he wanted a child. A different kind of love. Practical. He sat in the tub, his legs stretched out, arms at his sides. With no one in the house, he felt strangely abandoned. He started to shiver like he did as a boy, waiting for his mother to pick him up from swim practice. She was always late. He was always the last kid to leave. He hated competition. And trophies. He now admitted this to himself. He got out of the tub and dressed.

When Celine and Paulo returned from the beach, Jean-Paul ran out and hugged his son so hard the boy cried out, "Ow, Papa! It hurts." Celine looked at Jean-Paul wide-eyed. He smiled back.

⟶

It was their last evening at the villa. Jean-Paul had relented on the *ripiddu*, and they had demolished the volcano down to the last black grain of rice. All that remained was a pool of tomato sauce lava.

Evelyn, Celine and Paulo had long since gone to bed. The herbal fragrance of the macchia blew in from the surrounding hills—fir, myrtle, rosemary, thyme.

Alex tipped his head. "The cicadas have stopped."

"Probably because the resort turned the floodlights off."

"Why don't we have one last late-night swim."

They paddled idly in the illuminated water, cooler than the ambient air. Jean-Paul had forgotten to swim like that, without thought of distance or metres. They floated on their backs, or tried to, lamenting how men lack the built-in flotation that women enjoy. Alex got out first, and then Jean-Paul, shivering slightly. He tried to cover this up by joking about why there's no such thing as men's synchronized swimming because they'd all drown. Alex immediately picked up a towel and draped it around his son.

They sat in their deck chairs, wrapped in towels, puffing on Cohibas in the dark, like two old friends enjoying a cigar in celebration of somebody's birth.

Strangely Luminescent in the Dusk

The moon is a faint blue glow barely discernible in the oysterish sky. They reach the red brick building and rush up the stairway to the third storey. Attacus bolts the door from the inside. It smells like hot oven, things trapped in boxes. The long-ago past. A moth bashes itself against the dormer window. Adela opens the window to set it free. Across the way in another building, a toddler chants, "Numma, numma, numma, nah." They make out. This has become a regular thing, a way of forgetting. Adela runs her hands over the snake head tattoo on Attacus's bicep. He smells her skin.

"Del. Did you ever want to have kids?"

"Nah. Well, I don't know. You would've made a good dad, though." She lies back on the floor, arms spread over her head. "Oh Atty, I can feel again. That feeling—who said it—that stab right at the base of your spine. Unh." Attacus rolls over and rubs his woolly red hair into her belly.

"Del, you know what I like about you? You can make snow angels even when there's no snow." He flaps his hairy arms up and down, his long tongue hanging out like an unfurled party favour. Attacus is slightly crazy, but Adela loves him. She grabs his closest arm to stop the flapping.

"We're still on earth, Atty. Don't spread your wings just yet." Other than his bouts of melancholy and occasional drug use, Adela finds him irresistible, especially his tongue.

They don't know the attic has another occupant. A balding man who goes there with his portable stool and draws compound eyes on index cards, each labelled "The Eye." At other times he sketches butterfly genitalia which he carries with him in small vials meticulously labelled in elegant handwriting. They haven't noticed him hovering around corners, his white knee socks strangely luminescent in the dusk.

⌐

When they're not in the attic, they're sequestered at the Centre for Biogenetics—Port 1 for Attacus, Port 4 for Adela—undergoing observation for the Transgenetic Protocol: Lepidoptera transfer. They don't know if they're in the control group or the experimental group, and they don't really care. They signed up for the food and the money—survival. After treatments they recover at Adela's.

Night is their daytime, the moon their sun, and the city streets their domain. Adela has photophobia. Her life unfolds in the liminal light, like a cinema with a screen lit by a failing projector. It's one of the most common outcomes of people in the Port 4 trials. Which is why they're paid at a slightly higher rate.

During the day, the two of them avoid the city. Hungry, hollow-eyed people roam the streets, and the reflective surfaces of abandoned commercial buildings assault Adela's eyes. But by night, with only a few generators operating, the city is dimmer and the desperate people have retreated to the camps. Adela still remembers the daylight of her childhood: not a pale fire like these times but a dazzling orange mirror turned on your face, lighting you outside-in. And the evening smells—whiffs of dairy farms floating in from the outskirts, fresh-cut grass, scented wood smoke. She could almost *feel* the scents that marked out her life. Night is different now: diesel from generators, fast food, dog poo and reeking garbage, a seasonless hash. Yes, she has reduced vision, but this has only heightened her other senses.

It's early July. The second trial observation period is over. Adela has found a new route into the city that cuts through the derelict fish market. Attacus taught her how to navigate by consulting the sky, not the pavement. The market reeks of brine, piss and creosote. Under the buckled concrete, displaced people, rejected for the trials, sleep in makeshift tents in the former loading bays. The old Oyster Hall in the Craftsman Building has imploded. They pick up speed to get through the ruins as quickly as possible.

"Atty, your pants are too tight. I can hear them whistling."

"Whistling? Is it alluring, Miss Septentrionella my bella?"

"No. Fabric on fabric means *stridulation*."

"Stridu-what?"

"Rubbing body parts. Didn't they tell you about that? Not too good for the genitals."

"Yeah, but it's part of the plan." Atticus rubs his head with his hairy hand. "Del, how is it you've got wonky eyes but ultrasonic hearing?"

"Because, unlike you and your waxy gummed-up tufts, I actually clean my ears more than once every ten years."

As they turn into Becker Street, Atticus senses someone lingering in the shadows, but says nothing. He knows that up ahead is Adela's favourite microgarden and it would spoil it for her.

It's spoiled anyway. Adela's in front of the metal gate, which is secured by a new padlock. "I can't believe they're locking it! One little patch of green and loveliness. What's here to steal?" Waves of jasmine and apple blossom drift over the gate. She closes her eyes and inhales the scent, which may or may not be artificial. Grasping the gate wire, she steps up onto the bottom rail to peek into the garden. A powerful floodlight blasts on.

Behind them, a trash can crashes to the pavement. Attacus pulls Adela away from the glaring light. A fox emerges from the alley with a Chinese food container in its mouth, one of the recent immigrants from the dying forests that now stalk the back streets of the metropolis. It stares at them with its reflective eyes, assessing their threat level, then darts away with its takeout prey.

Attacus takes Adela's hand to continue their walk. "Just the local wildlife."

"Atty, light hurts now. Those huge yellow lamps at the Centre feel like banshee screams piercing my eyeballs. And the flicker of fluorescents drives me insane. I can't stand being like this. It's cut out whole swathes of what my life could be. If I have one anymore."

Attacus rubs his money fingers together. "Anything to help the Republic." His eyes are turned toward a boarded-up building to the right. "You see that guy? He's been following us." Adela squints into the blackness.

"Well, I don't see anything, Mr. Paranoid. He's probably just some shmuck that likes to walk at night."

"I'm telling you, it's him. The stalker. The man from the shadows. He's probably reporting into his implant device." Adela laughs. "Del, can't you see him? He's got something with a long handle tucked under his arm. Looks like a fishing net. Maybe he's moonlighting as a feral dog catcher. Or a fox catcher." The man goes into Blavdak's Diner, a blast of retro fluorescence with a neon sign that blinks—*Ice Cold Drinks! Ice Cold Drinks!* At a table by the window, a dark-haired man spoons cherry pie into a petulant girl's red candy mouth.

"Gah! It's too bright for me, Atty."

They move out of view to a side street to watch the bald man. Food smells waft from the diner—greasy hamburgers, liver and onions, fries—but don't entice them. Attacus almost never eats and Adela's preferred food is sugary pop, the more vivid the colour the better (both clinical outcomes from the trials). They see the man in profile. His net is propped up against the table. It looks more like a butterfly net than one to catch foxes. One last tangle of fried onions dangles from his upheld fork. He eats in slow motion, as if simultaneously writing a novel in his head. When finished, he removes his napkin from his lap, folds it into a triangle, smoothes a twenty-dollar bill on the table as if petting a cat and heads out the door.

They follow him. He heads straight to "their" building and enters. A weak light goes on at the first floor. They ponder the coincidence, wait a few more minutes, then decide to risk going to the attic. They remove their shoes before going up the stairs. Someone has been there. In the corner under the eaves sits a large ovoid thing, a shiny mahogany-coloured casing about the size of an infant. A sculpture? It makes her think of an Egyptian sarcophagus. She touches it gently and feels the whorls of her own fingerprint. "Oh, oh," she whispers.

"It looks like a cocoon," Attacus reaches out to lift it.

"No, don't!" Adela pulls him back. "There's something inside it." They both lean in, searching for features on the brownish covering.

Attacus pouts. "I wanna see what's going on in there."

"It's developing. Just like us, silly."

Had the bald man put it there? Or had it somehow come from them? They agree to watch over it.

⟿

Over the next two weeks they visit the cocoon regularly, confident in its unfolding processes, protective of it. It comforts them, hints at some kind of future that they themselves have been denied. It makes the other world, the trials, fall away. Sometimes it seems to rock back and forth, especially if the floor is warm or the sun shines on it. Other times it twitches. Over time the shell becomes taut. There are etchings on the outside, outlines of veins and mouthparts, whether insect or human it's not clear. On one occasion a folding table and stool appear in the room. There's a vintage metal pencil sharpener, expertly sharpened pencils, and index cards covered in small, cramped writing and scribbles (more insect eyes). A hasty sketch of the cocoon is tacked onto the wall. Attacus reads the words "Crispr-Cas9."

"Genome editing." Attacus leans over an open journal full of notes.

"'... select Lepidoptera'–that's moths and butterflies... 'Moth-eye silicon film increases conversion of photons.' Increases photons. Hey, that's just what you need, Del."

"Yeah, like a year ago."

"Yep."

Adela feels uneasy that a stranger has breached their space.

Attacus flips the journal cover over. "Dr. Aba Movlinkiov. I believe we are squatting in some genius geneticist's think-space."

For a stretch of time—first quarter moon to waning crescent—they can't go to the attic. Attacus is ill but refuses to report to the clinic for biogenetically reassigned clients as he is supposed to. He says he's not himself, his skin is crawling, dry and tight, but it's not the meth (technically, forbidden). He regrets signing up for the trials, even if the money is good. Adela can see that his hair has thinned. He sleeps most of the day in her windowless pod in the East Zone, curled up, listening to the ripped Republic flag flap in the wind outside. She assures him he will get better, but all he replies is, "I mourn because the world is so untrustworthy."

"Excuse me. Can I sit here?" Adela pulls her hood off and slides into the booth at Blavdak's Diner. The bald man with the white knee socks indicates with his right hand to sit down.

"You're shadowing us, aren't you?"

"Yes."

"I'm Adela. Well—*now* I am."

"Yes. I know. I named you. Although I didn't know it was you at the time. You were only Subject 67-4 and your friend was Subject 34-1."

Adela glances past the bald man's shoulder to a window seat where a dark-haired gentleman is feeding cherry pie to an adolescent girl as if they're locked in an inappropriate Sisyphean romance.

The bald man leans forward and says in a whisper, "You've taken a risk coming into the low-security zone alone. Be aware that there are Republic agents lurking everywhere."

"So—why?" she whispers back.

He extends a hand to her. "Abram." There's a strange scale-like pattern on the top of his hand that bristles when she grasps it. In the corner, the dark-haired gentleman places a cherry into the small 'o' of the girl's mouth where she holds it, looking back at him with ambiguous girl-woman's eyes. "I am the former director of the Centre for Biogenetics. I was assigned the position under duress. It was not my intention to harm you."

"You're the one conducting the Lepidoptera Protocol?"

"Yes. No. I was. I named you *Adela septentrionella*, after the fairy longhorn moth. Your friend is *Attacus atlas*, the snake's head moth. I am Dr. Aba Movlinkiov."

"You're the one—"

"Yes. It is my own trial, the cocoon. There were other ways to conduct the research. Human stem cell transfer to Lepidoptera was my preference."

"I think my friend Atty is dying."

"That is possible." His eyes dart out the window. "I am going to lock the attic from now on. I will not return to it. But you can both still go there. It is my gift. Here is a key. I must go." He hastily throws a twenty-dollar bill on the table and flees.

A few days later, Atty says he's better (he isn't). They go back to see the cocoon, but Adela mentions nothing about meeting Dr. Movlinkiov.

It's a moonless night. The Milky Way leaks across the sky. Stars spill from the centre of the galaxy like granules of snow. Deep within the galaxy's core, beyond the scope of the human eye, is a massive black void whose discovery had been cause for much joy in the astronomy world. At least, before interest waned in that discipline. Attacus's forehead is streaming with sweat. He wipes it with his hand. Sweat beads cling to his upper lip. Yesterday he received his final payment from the Centre. Two thousand Republic dollars, which weren't worth that much. A few synthetic beef burgers.

"My knowledge is just tiny pinpricks of light on a gigantic black sheet of ignorance," he says sadly, face up to the sky. "I wish I could launch myself into space."

"Atty, we *are* in space."

"Good point."

They walk slowly past Blavdak's Diner, mourning the days they could ingest hills of French fries and *real* burgers smothered in bacon and cheese. Inside, diners stare at their reflections in the window as if they don't recognize themselves. The odd Sisyphean couple are at the window booth with their eternal slice of cherry pie. The geneticist is not there tonight.

Adela fingers the copper plaque with the name "Fabre" on their building. It's surprising no one has stolen it yet to sell on the black market. They walk up one flight of stairs, Attacus hunched over as if he has shrunk during his illness, grasping the wrought iron banister, his face ashen. "Oh, man, Del. Not sure I can make it."

Adela puts her hand around Atty's waist to help him. He has to rest for several minutes every fourth step. At the landing she inserts Dr. Movlinkiov's key in the door. Atty stands by, panting, leaning on the wall.

"Del. Gotta sit down. Not feeling... good." Atty collapses into the battered armchair. Adela approaches the cocoon. The pointed tip is peeled back.

"Atty. It opened." Atticus does not answer. Adela peers inside but sees nothing. She looks to the window. Above it, clinging to the wall, is an enormous moth with a thorax of smooth ivory skin. "Atty! Its eyes are the same colour as mine, just kinda different." She leans in closer. "It has long feathery antennae that look exactly like your hair! Atty? Atty...."

Music from a Strange Planet

They call her Lucky Bee, or Xingyùn mifēng, her father's Chinese nickname for her. Here are five things you need to know about Lucky Bee:

1. Her bangs are cut that way (like a half-pulled window blind) because her grandmother uses a ruler.
2. No one may touch her body without prior permission.
3. Her favourite colours are magenta (F# major) and viridian (B minor).
4. She first learned how to play the viola "from the vibrating strands that fall down through the air."
5. The one thing you don't want known about yourself will be known by Lucky Bee in your first meeting. (As a toddler, she often blurted out startlingly prescient statements about people at the dinner table. This soon dwindled off when she saw the mildly horrified looks on her parents' faces.)

She is, indeed, a girl with particular talents. But she also has chocolate smears at the corners of her mouth and a hop and a skip to her step.

When Lucky Bee was six, her grandmother gave her a gift.

"Xingyùn mifēng, come here. I have something for you."

Lucky Bee put down her viola. On the coffee table there was a small antique cage of enamel and bronze with lively painted dragons on the corners.

"Look. Yeh Yeh's name is on the bottom. He bring it all the way from China to Vancouver."

The girl bent down to view the faded script of her grandfather's name. When she touched the cage's cool frame, she experienced it as the flavour of fresh lime juice. "Thank you, Mah Mah," she said and lifted up the cage by its hook.

"Wait." Her grandmother pulled a tiny, decorated box from her sweater pocket and slid open one side, tilting it through the door of the cage. A cricket ventured out slowly.

"Does he sing?"

"Yes, but not yet. He need to feel safe. You put him in the window where he can see outside."

Lucky Bee's mother was in the kitchen doorway listening, wiping her doughy hands on her Iron Chef apron, scowling at her mother-in-law. Things from the old country drove her around the bend. She was Helen. A non-hyphenated Canadian.

Lucky Bee named the cricket Li-Qin, beautiful stringed instrument. She talked to the cricket. It told her things—when it would rain, which neighbour would win the lottery, when the Canada geese would return in spring—in words that sounded like lyrics from a song. Li-Qin was infallible, it seemed. Li-Qin also knew when circumstances were con-figuring themselves for impending disaster. His silence was a warning.

⌐

One week after Lucky Bee got Li-Qin, she carried him in his cage to the park. They sat on a picnic bench with a view to the mountains.

There was a slant to the light that made everything angular, like a scream that had hung in the air for a moment and never been heard. Li-Qin had sung all the way from home but stopped when Lucky Bee put the cage down. She looked around. There was a young man off to the left, underneath a maple tree. He was standing on a picnic bench. There was a thick rope hanging from a branch. He was trying to fit his head in the loop, but his pants kept sliding off his scrawny body. She ran over to him, clutching the cricket cage.

"Fuck off. I'm busy." The man had sores and bruises all over his arms. When she looked at them she could sense how tender they must feel to him.

"You can't do that. It will hurt the tree. And you'll hurt yourself."

"Fuck—" The man's pants dropped again. "Little girl, take your bird and get outta here."

"It's not a bird. It's Li-Qin. Listen. He says *you're beautiful, you're free.* He's a cricket. He's in a cage, but he's still happy."

"Fucking kid. Get the—" The man tried to push her away and fell off the bench, defeated. Lucky Bee sat with him on the grass for twenty minutes while he cried. When he left, she didn't let him take the rope.

On another occasion, when she noticed her neighbour Elspeth was not going outside anymore, she asked Li-Qin what to do. *Do the electric dance. There's more time than you think. Stick your face in a rose. Smell the pink.* She knocked on the old woman's door, holding the cricket cage. They all sat together in the rose garden, even though the roses had dropped their petals already. At first, the woman's voice sounded to Lucky Bee like an old song squeezed into wax, but when the morning sun warmed it, it came back to life. Lucky Bee did a jerky dance to Li-Qin's lyrics and Elspeth spilled her tea. Their meetings became a weekly occurrence.

There were times when the girl believed that the artist Prince was speaking through her pet, but she kept this to herself. Her mother did not believe in such things. She would have waved her big dog-face oven mitts at Lucky Bee and scolded her for thinking like that. What Lucky Bee's mother believed in was libraries. Nevertheless, a lot of other people did believe something auspicious was going on in the Chan household. And they started to come to the house to ask the cricket about marriages, illness and business ventures. But the girl answered only if Li-Qin did.

Lucky Bee liked music. She loved Prince. But she also loved Respighi and Messiaen. And Scelsi. The power of a single note. In the same year she got Li-Qin, Lucky Bee composed a sonata for viola titled "Music from a Strange Planet," inspired by the periodic convergence of cricket choruses. This, after just one year of studying composition. Although it baffled her parents, it won the Zehman-Walter Young Composer's Award and was performed at the Hamilton International Chamber Music Festival in front of an audience of two hundred. At the award presentation, she spoke only four words into the mic: "All. Sounds. Are. Music." Her father grinned and said the piece sounded to him like a hundred lathes all cutting through metal at the same time. Her mother said, "You know, people all over the world eat crickets. It's called entomophagy."

Lucky Bee always looked as if she had passed through the present moment and was already rushing to the threshold of the new, of what was yet to unfold. She saw the potentiality of all acts and was therefore never surprised at outcomes. Li-Qin merely enhanced this trait. She did play with toys, although not necessarily in the way other children did. She had dolls named after musical modes: Ionia, Doria, Lydia. They were neither her "babies" nor her charges to order around. She set them up in tableaus and listened to their conversation, each doll speaking in the pitches of her corresponding scale. Her collection of matchbox cars was the envy of the neighbourhood boys. While theirs were chipped and scratched from being raced down driveways, crashed, and thrown at walls, Lucky Bee's were in pristine condition. Each car, to her, had its own "flavour." Volkswagen van: pumpkin pie; Jeep Renegade: grape juice; Datsun 501: burnt toast. Some of the cars were from her father's collection, and the rest her father had ordered expressly for her. He even built her a diorama of their neighbourhood. Lucky Bee did not like the cars for their singularity but for their collective effect. She spent hours arranging and rearranging them in specific scenarios, captured in moments of suburban activity. Sometimes she heard it as music.

On that frosty October morning when Li-Qin suddenly went silent upstairs, Lucky Bee was alone in the basement, engrossed with her cars. She had the grocery truck pulling away from the stop sign at Victoria and East Thirty-Sixth, then her parents' grey Nissan hurtling through the intersection, spinning around sideways. It was not until after the accident that someone noticed the coincidental configuration.

Lucky Bee's mother and father are buried side by side at the Mountain View Cemetery with both their Chinese and Canadian names on the gravestones, much against her mother's wishes, although she was hardly in a position to complain. Lucky Bee does not visit them, but her grandmother does.

"Xingyùn mifēng, I am going to *fan dei*, the graveyard. Your mother and father are lonely."

Lucky Bee's parents could never really claim her in life, and even in their death, she exists in a parallel time whose lines don't intersect theirs. Neighbours thought the girl abnormal for never grieving their deaths. But she had already grieved for them, the moment she was born.

The Vigil

He had come after work, as he always had for the last nine years, to see his aging mother. Except that this time it was urgent. The staff admired Gerald. They called him "the Golden Boy" even though he was neither a boy nor golden. He was a clerk in an auto parts wholesaler. They thought his filial diligence was an act of love.

He entered the hot room and dragged a chair over to her bed. She lay immobile, as she had for the last year, as if fixed on some far point of eternity. The wall clock jerked to 6:00. The TV was on. A Malaysia Airlines Boeing 777 had disappeared into oblivion over the southern Indian Ocean. Nobody knew why or how. The networks liked a good mass death story. His mother, too. She had always thrived on high drama and tragedy. TV was like a drug to her. He turned back to her, or what was left of her. Certainly not much of her brain. He noticed an insect slowly stepping up her left cheek. It looked like an assassin bug or maybe a shield bug, the ones that used to ruin her tomato plants and make the fruit bitter. She was now too insensate to react to it. He watched it lift each thin leg mechanically up the landscape of her pale skin. Its antennae tracked the textures of her face, the mole beside her mouth, the flaky corners of her nose. He thought back to that boy in grade four, when they gathered around as he pulled the legs one by one off a daddy-long-legs, watching it twitch. Randy was his name, a compulsive liar, yet well-liked because his lies were so outrageous they were entertaining. The one about his grandfather dying on the Titanic was especially ambitious. When he spoke, foamy saliva would gather at the corners of his mouth. Gerald's mother used to lick her index finger and dab down some errant hair on Gerald's head with her saliva. The past felt to him like an impossibly long tunnel that would suffocate him if he ventured into it too far. And yet, he never felt he was living in anything resembling a present.

"John, you're on-site in Perth. Tell us where Flight 370 is suspected to have gone down in the Indian Ocean."

The field reporter stood beside a vast body of water waving his hand toward a vaguely defined area, as if this gesture could encompass the great mystery of death.

A nurse peeked in through the ward door and, seeing Gerald there with his mother, gave him a benevolent smile and left them alone. The bug was traversing the side of his mother's nose in the direction of her right eyebrow. Disorderly eyebrows, not the over-plucked drawn-on clown arches that she used to have.

In his mind's eye he could see her in front of the mirror in her bedroom, removing the dauber from the purple decanter and dabbing the perfume all over her neck and shoulders. He associated that perfume with a pervading unhappiness, a fragrance his mother applied to forget or deny something, to protect herself. Then she would take up the brown eye pencil and draw on her clown eyebrows where her real eyebrows should have been if she hadn't pulled them all out. She would sing when she did this, quavering, sentimental songs. But now it seemed her body was reclaiming her, reverting to its wild state.

As a boy, he'd fallen in love with his friend Larry's mother. She had real eyebrows. And eyes that let you in, made you feel everything was going to be alright. She often sang when she was out in the garden, old lilting tunes like "The Tennessee Waltz" and "Allegheny Moon," in a voice that felt to him like a long, cool drink in summer.

At age fifty-five, out of the blue, he'd started taking singing les-sons. He didn't tell anyone at work, but he did tell his mother. She disapproved, as if anything that increased his pleasure caused her an inverse diminishment. His voice teacher was patient, trying to help him find that beautiful core of sound. But he could only rarely access it and, for a brief moment when he did, it brought with it a freedom freighted with terror. She had suggested he try singing the Handel aria "Ombra mai fu," a simple but touching song sung by King Xerxes about his fondness for a plane tree that has provided him with shade through turbulent years. Gerald liked it but broke down every time he sang it. He never understood why.

CNN bombarded the screen with elaborate graphics and maps riddled with directional arrows showing the plane's purported tra-jectory. "No one really knows what happened here," said a female talking head. He got up and turned off the television. The bug had reached his mother's hairline, interpreting the unruly thicket of hair by sweeping its antennae back and forth like a blind man's cane. It hesitated, as if asking itself, what is this obstacle? Where should I go next? He finally flicked it from his mother's scalp, then stood staring at her for a long time. She was very still. A rhomboid patch of light lay across her body. A sickly scent of almonds and old books hung in the air. Without saying goodbye, he left the room. The beginnings of an immense space opened inside him.

⌒

He got in the car and drove away. By the time he reached the free-way on-ramp his body started to shake, like a train was driving through him from the soles of his feet, up through his calves, thighs, gut, chest, neck and out through his hands. He gripped the steering wheel more firmly to control the tremor. His usual exit came up, but he drove right past it. A long, low moan formed deep in his bowels, a primal sound similar to the one Tibetan monks make when they chant, only not spiritual. At first, he didn't know it was coming from himself. He continued driving. He felt impelled to keep moving. The sound moved up, filling his chest cavity. A semi-truck began to tailgate him. It flashed its lights menacingly, bullying him to move over into the right lane. The sound reached his throat and changed into the howl of a wounded dog, a lonely masterless dog. It became so loud and frightening that he thought he might be turning inside out. He was the sound. The sound was him. And it was the ugliest, rawest, yet most resonant sound he had ever made in his life.

He pulled into the right lane, swung over onto the shoulder and stopped the car. He put his head on the steering wheel and emptied out an agony that felt very, very old. Snot poured out of his nose and dripped down on his lap, but didn't care, didn't stop to wipe it. He lived inside and through that sound, let it take him wherever was required until the moan lessened into sobs, then into huge heaving breaths that alternately exhausted and revitalized him. And then it stopped. He sat up, looked out through the windshield at the concrete overpass, the lamp standard, the highway speed sign, not comprehending what they were. The connection between his eyes and his brain was temporarily shut off. Only when a red car whizzed by on the overpass did he come back to awareness.

He pulled back onto the highway, a little too slowly, and took the next exit, Linn River. He didn't care. About two kilometres down the road was a small park. He pulled in. Since it was a weekday around dinnertime, no one else was there. He walked the gravel path past the forlorn and outdated playground. There were graphic signs warning about the undertow in the river. They'd been placed strategically on the trailhead so you couldn't avoid them. He looked at the illustrations. Drowning people swirled like adult fetuses trapped in a turbulent womb. He'd seen a drowning victim once, a local boy who'd been pulled from a lake. The strange serenity on the boy's face had haunted him, and the thought of the boy's lungs filled with water. He walked on to the end of the path and stepped down to the river's edge. Leaves and twigs circled endlessly in whirlpools, making it look as if the river was going backwards. A blurred roar, almost blissful. He crouched down to feel the water. Deadly cold.

On the opposite bank was a towering cottonwood tree. He smelled its sap in the air. Balm of Gilead. It reminded him of the smell of his father's pipe. His father's smoking was a kind of language, a way of saying things to his wife that he preferred not to say out loud but instead inhaled through his pipe and transmuted into smoke which hung unresolved in the living room air. His mother would have stood there in her frumpy housedress, in a cloud of rancid perfume, unable to decode the situation.

The river rushed past. He took off his shoes and socks and stood in the water. He took a deep, unfettered breath, filling his lungs with air. He did it again. The day's last light illuminated the white bark of the cottonwood tree. King Xerxes and his plane tree. *Never was a shade of any plant dearer and more lovely, or more sweet.* He would work on that song until nothing but beauty came from his voice.

Be My Beloved

"... is that the chubby clay goddess with breasts like water balloons?" Margo rushes out of the university conference hall to the wooded back of the parking lot typing "yes" to her friend Juliette's question. It's three-thirty and the conference is over. Her lecture on contemporary practices in behavioural therapy went wildly off-topic. When she hits "Send," a man approaches, asking her to help him with the ticket machine. She takes him there and explains the steps. It seems odd that he couldn't figure out the machine. He walks with her to the back of the lot to place the ticket on his dashboard. His car is parked beside hers, and as they approach, he pops the trunk—by mistake, he says. When she turns to walk away he grabs her from behind, covers her mouth and pushes a needle into her thigh. She collapses into him, as if swooning. It might have looked romantic from a distance had anyone seen it.

⟶

"What?" Max had been perplexed at Margo's proposal earlier that week.

"Sologamy. It's a way of staking out the parameters, saying, 'This is my life and I'll live it to the fullest of my potential. I will honour and love myself.'"

"But Mags, you do that already. Why marry yourself? Why devote yourself to exclusion?"

"You're not excluded from my life, Max." Margo had subtly pushed the dogs to the side of the bed with her feet and put her head closer on Max's pillow. "This way, I get to have you *and* be me."

"But you are yourself with me."

"You think that."

"Geez, Mag, talk about 'cognitive distortion.' This sologamy thing's like upscale narcissism. I feel like you're rejecting me and trying to keep me at the same time. It's nuts."

"Nope. It's a done deal. Fortieth tomorrow! Ceremony the week after. That was my promise to me. Juliette helped me write the vow: 'I promise to be my own beloved....'" Max turned away from her. They'd ended up in a frosty non-truce.

Margo had not slept over that night.

———

She's in a spaceship, rocketing through darkness. It feels like a swarm of bats is circling her insides, but she can't vomit. There's a rag in her mouth. A ringing in her ears, like crazy tubular bells. The rocket lurches suddenly to one side, then slows. For a moment, a tiny room in her brain opens up: car trunk, not rocket ship. She tries to sequester it. But it slips away, and the space collapses.

———

Max's dogs have bolted and strain at the end of the leash, wrenching his leash hand. He lets them loose. They charge away from the crumbling cliffs to the water's edge to explore something in the shallows. Probably something maimed and vulnerable, knowing his dogs' instincts. Margo is incommunicado about her birthday dinner. They were going to discuss what part he would play in the ceremony. Understanding Margo is like puzzling out sudoku, another thing he's bad at. All the possible combinations and permutations. Sologamy ceremony. Really? Who marries *themselves*? Juliette, who sees mutual love as some sort of weakness, probably planted the idea. It seems every time he and Margo get really close, Margo launches herself like a human missile miles away from him.

When they'd first met, he could picture her in every lovemaking configuration imaginable. They smashed lamps, made pictures fall off the wall, broke furniture. The dogs whined downstairs, locked in the TV room, unfamiliar with the feral in humans. But the closer he and Margo got, and the more they acknowledged each other as more than a source of sex, the more his fantasies crashed. He became tormented by how much or even if she loved him, and the torment drove him further into a needy kind of love. Initially, he'd thought she was wild and exciting. He was wrong. That was purely physical. Magnetism. Once the voracious lovemaking had worn off she appeared to him as wild in an entirely different way. The way a wild animal taken as a pet seems domesticated but then one day breaches the boundary fence and without so much as a glance back at its loving owner, vanishes back into the forest.

Max catches up with the dogs. The object of their fascination: a large jellyfish in a gelatinous state of disintegration, a once graceful, albeit brainless, creature reduced to a shapeless ooze. He clips the leashes back on and steers the dogs away from it.

Farther down the beach, a young couple walks a teeny Shih Tzu. It advances with balletic steps, stretching the retractable leash to its maximum. As the little dog nears, Max's Weimaraners perk up. He reins them in.

"Poppy!" The couple reel in their dog, too, away from Lily and Amy's slathering mouths. "Wow. What type of dogs are those? They're very elegant."

"Weimaraners," Max says. "They look gentle, but they're hunters. They'll chase and kill anything that remotely resembles prey." The Shih Tzu stands between the woman's legs, shuddering.

The couple smiles together, with the same smile, in the same jackets. As if they've merged into one blissful entity. His bachelorhood and devotion to his Weimaraners, which in secret he considers his children, is becoming embarrassing to him. He glances down at Lily with her pale blue eyes. *Very sensitive; hate being alone; like to be within touching range; intelligent; intense*—strange how people gravitate to dogs with their own characteristics. He's a lecturing family psychologist who can't even sustain a loving relationship. He hates Margo's sologamy ceremony idea. But he won't let her go.

The dogs drag something out of the bushes and fight over it. A small animal skull, with maggots wriggling in the strips of ragged flesh.

———————

She opens her mouth to scream but no sound comes out. It's black everywhere. Inside her head, inside the trunk. Black like a deep tunnel. The black where you can't feel the outline of yourself. Does she still have arms and legs? Paralysis. She can't sense her body. And her mind is like a specimen in a jar separated from its host body. The driver cranks on the radio. Hallucinations again. The music is rivers of molten chocolate dripping from the ceiling. Max is there. They move as one body, doing some kind of dance. He drops her in a dip. But her head's so heavy it falls off. Max laughs, picks it up and tries to put it back on her body. It's a cosmic laugh, like he's swallowed the entire universe then opened his mouth to let it spill out again. It's loud. She's worried it's being broadcast. But in fact, outside of her body it's silent.

5:47. "Fucking piece of crap!" The driver pulls over. The GPS screen had lured him onto an inland road going away from the ocean. He punches the GPS, turns it off and pulls a U-turn to get back to the main road, Juan de Fuca highway. The road gets bumpier, with washboard sections that toss the chassis from side to side. There's less traffic, except for the occasional motorcycle ripping past. He drives with one hand on the steering wheel, careening around the sharp curves. A blanket of fog obscures the strait.

There are brief moments for Margo when her predicament is clear. Why? Why her? Who is he? Could be a parolee. Classic reenactment phenomenon. Random or targeted? Then the strange cosmic otherworld descends again, like a messed-up psychedelic meditation on the nature of everything. She struggles with the zip tie in the dark, pulls her hands apart to break it, strains to twist her wrists from side to side. The exertion makes her hyperventilate, which she can't afford to do with her mouth gagged. There's only so much oxygen. She waits and tries again and bashes her head. Frustration leads to thrashing and kicking. Her feet are free. She could kick out the tail light. She slides to the back of the trunk and positions her right leg where she thinks the light cover is. Three kicks and it's broken.

———

6:25. A siren whines in the distance. It gives her hope. A steep down-hill pitches her back and forth inside the trunk. The siren passes. The car stops and the driver's door opens. She hears him on the phone, "Yeah I got her." She's terrified he's going to open the trunk and kill her. But she's also afraid of being left in the trunk. He drums his fingers on the top of the car as if he's planning something.

———

He strolls away from the car and flings Margo's purse over the bank. From his shirt pocket he lifts out an e-cigarette, taps it in his right hand, lifts it to his lips. He takes a long, sucking drag, exhales the vapour in two steady streams from his nostrils. He does this twenty times. Down below, waves smash against the rock cliff. The fog bank is now inching up the shoreline. He throws the empty cartridge into the endless tracts of salal and walks back to the car. Margo is sobbing inside. He bangs on the trunk twice. He knows the ketamine will only last so long.

———

"Hello Goddess of the Free World!" Juliette is doing the mockup for the sologamy cake. The long-time friends have an ongoing joke referring to each other as goddesses. "I just made the Willendorf woman for the top of the cake. It works with marzipan. Looks awesome! I'm baking raspberry *individual* mini cakes! Get it? Oh my god, this is going to be so fun. Friends forever, eh? Text me."

Max pauses the recording and goes back a few minutes. He and Margo always record their lectures and sometimes use them as podcasts on his website. They've got three years' worth now, going back to when they first met. But this morning's was different.

"A few weeks ago on a walk, I was standing at the observatory in a thick fog, and it occurred to me that cognitive-behavioral therapy focusses on rehabilitating the perpetrator and their difficulties with interpersonal trust. But where's recourse for the victim? What of the victim's own thought processes that are now distorted? Yes, the Thought Change Method has proven a success, with an average sex offender recidivism rate of only 3 percent in six years. But the victims remain traumatized and struggle to deactivate their situation-specific behaviours, often years later."

What first bothered Max about the talk was that he'd been with her on that walk and she'd never mentioned this shift in her thinking. They often discussed their inner processes. But this morning as he sat in the lecture hall, words came out of her mouth he was unprepared for: "I am one of those survivors." Why had she chosen to reveal something so personal to a group of strangers? Why did she not confide in him? He'd tried to elbow his way through the audience to speak to her after, but she'd slipped away.

6:44 p.m. The university parking attendant places a violation ticket on the windshield of Margo's Audi.

The air in the trunk feels cooler. Autumnal. Had she slept deeply? Overnight, or just for a few hours? Time has no meaning. This drug he injected—she feels her bodily fluids moving. Blood? Lymph? Could that be right? Her skin—maybe that's also the drug—feels strange, like it doesn't belong to her. Her eyesight is coming back—underwater vision, catfish eyes, eyes that aren't her eyes. She forgot she was supposed to stick her hands through the tail light to alert people. But there were no people.

She's curled up with her legs tucked in like she used to do at night in bed when she was a teenager. She never told anyone about the man who lured her and stripped her naked in his dark "booty call" basement. After that point in her life, and ever since, she'd wanted to be hard, uncrackable, impenetrable. Her career was based on reforming the perpetrator. Now she wanted to heal the broken psyches of victims like herself.

7:25 p.m. Max hesitates, holds his finger above the text box, then deletes the text. He calls instead so he can hear her voice. So he can tell her how he really feels for her once and for all. She doesn't answer. "Mags, if you're still mad about the other day and the sologamy stuff, I'll apologize. Just tell me whether I should keep the roast warm until you get here, if you're coming. Call me back." He adds "Love you," even though he knows she hates that phrase. His counter-proposal will have to wait.

———⟩

The air is even more chilling. But there's no way for Margo to get warmer. The car lurches back and forth recklessly, tossing her from side to side, forcing her to brace herself with her feet.

Then, without warning, impact.

———⟩

7:50. Max's idle phone sits on the dining table next to the candles and the envelope he hoped might change everything. Margo's silence feels palpable, like a withdrawal. The opposite of his intentions. The roast beef is cold. He drops it into the garbage and blows out the candles—four: one for each decade of her life. The dogs are coiled into each other on the couch, as if they've absorbed his grief.

———⟩

The car is still. Eerie silence. The driver's not getting out. If he does, she can bargain. If not, she'll fight. The paralysis is wearing off. She can feel her fingertips. Other areas of her body seem more alive. But things aren't connected. Portions of her body can't communicate with the other portions, as if those parts were an inoperative conjoined twin. She doesn't dare make a sound until it's safe.

—)

In the brush below the cliff, Margo's phone rings and goes to message. "Mags. I've decided to go away with the dogs for a few days just to—I don't know. Maybe we can meet up again when I get back. I won't be here for the ceremony. I love you."

—)

She has waited for what seems an eternity. The driver hasn't got out of the car. On the right-hand side of the trunk she's spotted a strip of fabric hanging down. Trunk release. The disintegrated parts of her struggle to reach it. She'll have to rotate 180 degrees. Lying flat on her back, she inches toward the strip. Her hands are still tethered but she's able to tug on the tab with her fingertips. The trunk pops open.

Light assaults her eyes. The air smells of soil, wood smoke, evergreens. The image from her hallucination comes back—dancing with Max, him trying to put her head back on, that cosmic laugh she wanted to live inside. A longing rises up through her body like a red-tinted moon, pushing through layers of resistance. At what point did she no longer believe in love between two people?

Where is Max? She does not want to be alone.

All she has to do to get out is elevate her body. Her legs are inert, so she uses her tethered hands to haul herself up and is able to flop over the edge of the trunk and onto the ground.

The driver's body is wedged between the steering wheel and the airbag. She remembers the web tattoo. Kent Penal Institution. The man who kept women in his cellar. As expert witness she'd done the violent-risk assessment.

⌐

Voices chatter. Time seems compressed, as if she's living several strands of her life simultaneously. She feels herself being lifted onto the gurney by the emergency responders. Someone places their hands tenderly under her head to adjust the pillow. Max? *Be my beloved.* She'll tell him as soon as she can.

The Mist-Covered Mountains

At the end of June, Dugald McEwen had put away his plumbing kit in the back shed, closed the door and clamped a rusty padlock on the latch. No more would he interact with the indescribable sludge that inhabited the drainpipes that inhabited the houses of the inhabitants of Cairloch. His lifetime of domestic plumbing disaster intervention had come to an end. He took his summer clothes, his Raleigh bicycle, and his old canister-shaped dog, Homer, and decamped for the summer (or maybe forever) to his ancestral stone house up in the Highlands. He'd also left behind a few bastard children (some with his signature dimple) scattered about the council and farther afield, conceived on couches, beds, and kitchen and bathroom floors in the more handsome and prolific years of his plumbing career, testament that the handyman allure was a potent antidote for housewifely ennui. In a certain era.

Dugald had thought he'd enjoy being alone in the Highlands. And he has spent time wandering the moor byways with Homer, trampling atop the millennial layers, but now he feels the dreaded retirement malaise everyone warned him about, a dark, gaping hole in the infinite expanse of his day. He mopes around the house, addressing family photos as if they might talk back to him—his aunt Enid with his mother at a picnic; his grandfather McEwen in uniform, posing beside his Triumph motorcycle; his brother, Rory, as a flame-haired infant—but the dead are resolutely silent. He wobbles on his Raleigh to the post box to look for his pension cheque. Eats at the pub until he can't look a codfish in the eye anymore. Switches to Chinese takeout and deli meat pies from the co-op until the kitchen counter is stacked with smelly cartons and metal pie plates. He goes to bed at nine and reads the same page (page ninety-seven) of *Moby Dick* over and over again until sleep overtakes him. Every morning the mute sun labours over Aellig Hill, and he wonders what the hell to do with the rest of the day. Until today.

He plunges his hand into one of the myriad boxes of the effluvia of his life and pulls out a cookbook, *The Scotsman's Scullery*. His mother's old, tattered copy, festooned with drips of oil, smeared spices and dried blobs of flour. A hundred and thirty-two recipes. On the spot, he decides to spend the year cooking every recipe in the book, from Baps and Cullen Skink to Tattie Scones. On the peat stove. It's Saturday, July thirtieth. He could finish by next May. The A section has been torn out (his father's ire when he found out his wife used his best whisky for the Atholl Brose). So Dugald starts with the Bs. First entry—Bannock.

⌒

Meanwhile in Toronto, a fly took up residence in a little girl's ear. In June, Pippa Brodie (in polite terms called a "kinaesthetic child") had woken up her mother and half the neighbourhood with blood-curdling screams and is now recovering from a fly in her ear. "Common housefly," said the presiding emergency room doctor, but was corrected by an intern who said definitively that it was a tachinid fly (much hairier than a housefly, and with red eyes like a pair of Ray-Bans). As a result of this trauma, Pippa now appears to be sporadically psychic. She draws pictures of a simple house in the Scottish moors and claims she lives there. She describes the surrounding countryside, the roads, the furniture in the house, and even "her" chair where she sat when the roof collapsed in 1807. Her mother, Robin, sent her to a psychologist, thinking the girl might have knowledge of a previous life. Perhaps the fly's persistent buzzing somehow rerouted her daughter's brain circuitry, creating a link to someone else's memories. Once the therapy proved inconclusive, her mother, who believed in taking to heart her daughter's "hallucinations," had decided to haul her off to Scotland for an exploratory tour.

⟶

"STOP!! STOP!! STOP!!"

Pippa jumps out of the car, sniffs the air ostentatiously, strides forcefully up the front stairs of a house a half block away from Dugald's, then freezes. She comes back down, leaps back in the car and says, "Keep going, Mom." It's Saturday, July thirtieth. They've already covered most of Aberdeenshire and had three false alarms. Her mother is beginning to think this whole thing is a bad idea. Maybe Pippa read somewhere about the Highlands and merged this with the scant information Robin had on her Scottish birth mother.

Pippa rolls down the car window and thrusts out her nose like a dog. "Stop. Stooooop!!!" She sits upright in her seat, eyes wide and crazy. "We're here. I smell it."

"Smell what?"

"The baking, the oven things, the bun smell. It's coming from that house with the long driveway." Part of her memories includes olfactory hallucinations of pipe smoke, dog fur and fresh baked bread. Her mother eases into the winding drive and parks. Pippa rushes up Dugald's front path and knocks forcibly on the door. In the kitchen, Dugald is trying not to burn the bannock on the round griddle, swearing blue murder at the smoky peat fire. He quickly moves the griddle to the hearth to answer the door.

"Hi, I know you."

"No, ye doant." Dugald has white flour on one cheek.

"Yes, I do."

"No, ye doant, lass."

"You're the one who crashed your Mini Cooper into the pub!"

Dugald slumps against the doorframe as if he's been shot by a firing squad.

"No, I'm noat. That was my father, Robert McEwen."

"Can I come in?" she says, elbowing Dugald aside, walking into his living room and straight up to his dog, which she bends down to sniff. "This is not the dog I smelled. Mine smelt like warm milk and leather."

"Might be you were smellin' an old milk cow. They used to keep them right in the house."

"You smell like a goat," she says to Dugald and sits herself down in "her" chair.

"Robin Brodie." The girl's mother rushes over the threshold and extends her hand. The man has a bit of a pong. "This is Pippa. Sorry, she just barged in." Robin explains the recovered "memories."

The name "Brodie" sticks in Dugald's head.

Pippa springs up to reach for an old clay object on the bookshelf. "What's this?"

"Granny McEwen's pipe."

"Ladies don't smoke pipes!"

"They did in the old days. She was a canny, solid gran. Worked every day of her life."

"This looks like my mom! What are those things on their backs?"

"That's my da and his sister with baskets of peat, somethin' ye dug out of the moors."

"What's moors?"

Robin pulls her daughter back into the chair.

They stay for bannock and jam. Dugald patiently explains to the girl how the peat stove works. As Pippa and her mother leave by the front door, Pippa shouts back, "And we'll come back on Sunday, too!" Dugald nods and runs *The Scotsman's Scullery* index through his head.

⌒

From the moment Robin had driven away yesterday, Dugald knew exactly what he would make for the little girl: Bonny's Fruit Slice. But nobody in their right mind ever called it that.

"And now I've baked a special thing for ye, lass, that every girl in Scotland has ate." Dugald brings out the dish and slices a huge chunk each. "Fly Cemetery." Pippa's eyes light up as she raises her fork.

"Really? With flies? Sweet. I had a fly in my ear!"

"Uh, no. There's no flies. Just raisins and currants that look like dead flies."

Robin rolls her eyes at Dugald.

Pippa had arrived brandishing a treasure from her grandma Margaret—a rare insect in amber, apparently from Scotland. Robin had given it to her to take along to Aberdeen as a kind of talisman. It was the only keepsake Robin had from her mother after she was given up for adoption. After the fly pie, Pippa takes the keepsake from her knapsack and hands it over.

When Dugald peers into the yellowish globe, past the scorpion-looking thing and into its prehistoric interior, he remembers one just like it, and a young wife named Morag, or Mairi, or Mag, with shapely legs and a voice like a trickle in a mountain creek. He'd never seen such tidy plumbing spaces. Not one fleck of silt or goo, no piles of dead beasties nor sour washcloths. He remembers their romping on the couch (oh, the atomic energy unleashed in that woman!) and his foot knocking over the end table, which sent the amber thing flying. They met a few times after but he hadn't seen her since. "And to think that one drop of pitch could stop a beastie in its tracks for millions of yairs," is all he can manage to say to Pippa before handing it back shakily.

"Do you think it's a midge?" Pippa hurls out factoids about the Scottish midge, informing them that the one that bites most is "Culcoides *im-punc-ta-tus.*"

"Good name," Dugald quips. "Punchy," and suggests they go outside and meet some. Pippa sprints out the back door.

"It's strange. She's doing things here she would never do at home. She's never talked about insects before...."

"It's the fresh Highland air."

They take Dugald's private path till it converges with the public one higher up. Homer comes along, too, poking his snout into crevices. Pippa runs ahead, windmilling her arms crazily.

"My brother and I had a time of playin' all over these hills. Last week I had a man trespassin' about. Wants me to lease the moors for a windmill farm. With the cash I could live the life of a minted baron."

"Would you do that?"

"Moors are a lonely place."

Robin and Dugald tread the spongy ground, inhaling the heathery piney scent.

"All this takes hundreds or thousands of yairs to develop. At the bottom, it's a slow-draining sink. Those peat men and women they've found there, some with their heads bashed in, presairved for all eternity. God knows it could be one of my own ancestors. Pickled like a leather satchel!"

Robin takes a deep breath. "The light here is lovely and clear. Everything is so sharply defined."

"Aye. Makes a good photo. My brother was one for the camera. He would get his knickers in a knot when once every five yairs the sun came out and he had to change the wee dial. Me, I just look with my own eyes." He surveys the undulating hillocks. "Over these sea pastures... all that we call lives and souls, lie dreamin', tossin' like slumberers in their beds."

"Oh. Robbie Burns?"

"No. Herman Melville. I've been reading *Moby Dick* for forty yairs and I still have nae finished. The only reason I know that line is I had to write it a hundred times for detention."

"Which means you were a bad boy."

"Aye." They swat away a cloud of midges. Pippa is charging up through the grass and heather. "There's a scientist fella in Finland can name any one of these biting beasties just by the very hum of its wings. I've got an agreement with the little buggers: they can hover but nae bite. Garlic and Marmite's the way. Although it's a bit heady for company."

Robin tells Dugald that Pippa took out every book in the library about Scotland. She read about Scotland's flora and fauna.

"She thought it was great how the ptarmigans changed to white for the snow. But she was particularly fascinated by the midge."

"Well, the midges will be very interested in her," said Dugald.

Pippa is high above them now.

"Look at her go!"

"Pippa operates on pure instinct."

Robin stops to take in the view. They have reached a plateau. Below them on the slopes, purple swathes of heather unfold amidst the lichened granite. "It smells heavenly."

"It's the *fraoch*, the heather. Likes the soil thin and meagre. Like a bachelor thrivin' on bread crusts."

"My mother was born somewhere in the Highlands. She left for Canada at twenty-one. That's all I know. It's so nice to be here in the moors. I didn't really expect them to exist anymore. I was hoping Pippa might grow out of all this past life business, but now I'm glad we're here."

"The land goes way back. My father and his da wair peat diggers. Dirty job. Digging trenches, spading the bricks and a pitchy fire burning all day in the house. Now the fancy gardeners don't want the peat. Dooznt grow back. And the capitalists want to put up wind fairms."

"I never knew my father." Above them, Pippa has vanished in a veil of mist. Above that, the bare mountains look violet in the afternoon light. Robin calls up to Pippa to come back. "We should be going now."

After weeks of solitude and soggy takeout, Dugald isn't ready to let his visitors go.

"How about a bite at The Auld Dog?"

⁓

When they step into the restaurant's dim murk, everyone turns and stares.

Dugald whispers, "Yer newcomers. Although you Canadians are always considered part of the clan."

Robin and Dugald drink the local ale. Dugald breaks into song and his voice is quite good, even on the high notes. Despite his paunchy regular-guy appearance, he is a man of charming surprises.

"Wow! What was that?"

"Chì Mi na Mòr Bheanna, The Mist-Covered Mountains."

"What language?"

"Scottish Gaelic."

"It sounds like *Lord of the Rings*. I like it," Pippa says.

"Now's yair turn, Robin."

"I don't know any Scottish songs. Or any songs."

"Sure ye do, everyone has a song in them. A tune ye know from heart."

"I do!" Pippa stands beside the table and cranks out "Somewhere Out There." Other customers clap.

Dugald is impressed. "She's a regular ham. You've roused the whole place now, Pippa." He thinks about how sometimes people who aren't your family feel like they could be your family. And sometimes they're better than your own family.

When they part, Dugald invites them to come by on Monday. And to teach an old Scotsman a Canadian tune.

Monday. The three of them sit on the back patio, eating Bread and Butter Pudding. Homer lies at Robin's feet. Inside Dugald's head, "The Hockey Song" reverberates.

"We're leaving Wednesday. Pippa's got a dance recital in a week."

"Ye could come again in fall. I'll be cookin' the Ds and Es then. Or next spring. The moor's a sight to see in spring. Streams so clear it's like looking in a mirror at yourself, back in time, like a stranger that ye know but ye doant know how ye know him."

"I'd like that. There's something about this place...."

"There's spirits in us who've lived in other times, other places."

After they leave, Dugald finds the amber globe on the kitchen table with a scribbled note. "To Mr Makyewan from Pippa—" That was it, plus a midge squished flat on the page, which may or may not have been part of the message.

Dugald polished the amber globe which now sits on the shelf of family portraits. He has Pippa pegged for someone who would delight in smashing things up. And so Tuesday afternoon's recipe is Broken Biscuit Cake, next recipe in the Bs. Their last day together.

"See, in the auld days ye could buy mixed-up, broken biscuits for cheap. Then we made a cake of it. Which is what you and I are goan to do and you're goan to pound the biscuits up." As Dugald opens the cookbook, a handwritten note falls out. "A love poem. That was a long ways back," Dugald says.

Robin bends down to pick it up, and as she hands it to Dugald he sees flecks of orange leaves in her green eyes, a flock of migrating golden plover passing by, like scenes in a fossil. He feels a warm glow deep in his belly. She smiles back. Dugald slips the note back into the cookbook.

"Don't you have a wife?" asks Pippa, biting into a piece of Broken Biscuit Cake while scratching Homer's ear.

"No, luv."

"So you don't have kids."

"No."

"None?"

"Not a one." As soon as he answers, he feels utterly lonely. But when he looks into that impertinent face across from him, he feels a flutter in his chest.

Pippa squints, leans forward, looks him square in the eye.

"Why?"

"Pippa, stop it! She's exactly like her father—rude and impetuous—which is why I decided to be a single mother." Robin sighs.

Dugald leans closer to Pippa. "Me mam said someone put a curse on me."

"But I know how we can get rid of it! We need one horse's head, three toads, six dandelions and some of your hair." Dugald runs his hand across his half-bald head.

"Oh, it's a wee bit late for that I think."

"Pippa!"

As they get up to leave, Pippa takes the clay pipe out of her pocket and asks retroactively, "Can I have this?" Her mother scolds her for being so rude, but Dugald doesn't hesitate a second.

"Sure, ye can. You've claimed it, haven't ye? And I'm sure Granny McEwen won't be missing it," he says, activating his dimple.

"You could be my dad! I wish I could live here." Pippa collapses back into the antique armchair and pretends to puff on the pipe.

"It seems to me, ye already have, luv."

Sing Fly Mate Die

Truth be told, Dave had never won a contest in his life. Not even two bucks on a scratch ticket. In fact, he'd never really won at the "game of life" at all. Failing computer business, average looks (bulgy eyes), and a two-thunk name—Dave Dunn—that sounded like a letdown. But one raffle ticket later, he's off to Missouri for a romantic getaway at Ziemsenn Vineyard Inn, in the historic German wine town of Hermann. Except that he's single. Always has been. And he doesn't drink wine.

In his mind he calls the trip "The Last Stand." The only thing he knows about Missouri is that it's home to one of the greatest baseball teams ever. For the overnight in St. Louis, he books a cheap motel under the name Dunn Davidson (which he thinks sounds better than his real name), arriving on the second of May 2011. As he lies on the king-size mattress at the Sleep Inn, he looks up at the ceiling and wonders if he's been more unhappy than he realized. Nothing beyond the frayed motel curtain interests him. He eyeballs the box of sleeping pills he brought. Five p.m. Pops three in his mouth.

He wakes with a start in the early morning, the sun barely up. His head feels like an overstuffed burrito. Checks his watch: 5:00 a.m. It sounds like someone outside is wielding a giant dentist's drill. A buzzy hovering sound. Like a B-movie spaceship. It's not a machine, not an airplane, but something infernal and urgent. Driven by irritation, he puts on his jacket and goes out to investigate. The noise—like thousands of tiny high-pitched instrument warning tones all screaming at once—comes from a wooded park about five blocks from the motel. It's like nothing he's ever heard before in his life. Its otherworldly weirdness draws him in.

In the park the ground becomes crunchy, like walking on inch-deep walnut shells. Hundreds of bugs are emerging from the ground, every square foot littered with their brittle shed skins. They crawl up the trees. The trunks are covered in them. And the sound: like a crackling bonfire, or a gigantic bowl of amplified Rice Krispies. Dave stops to take it all in. A young man with a bandana around his head steps out of the bush. Dave is afraid for a moment that he's a creep or maybe just looking for some action, but the guy looks too focussed to be dangerous.

"Dude, be careful where you step! They're coming out in the thousands."

"Uh, yes, never seen anything like it," Dave answers.

"I knew Brood Nineteen was gonna be big. But not this big. Are you from CicadaWatch group?" The guy has intense, piercing eyes.

"No, I'm just here for...." A romantic spa getaway. Dave chooses not to disclose his purpose.

The young man doesn't wait to hear Dave's response as he shouts over his shoulder. "We're meeting at seven a.m. outside the park, Clayton entrance. Check *CicadaMania* Twitter feed! They got Wi-Fi at Blueberry All-Night Café." He points away from the park perimeter. "Wilson Avenue. Sign with a giant blueberry on top." His voice trails off.

Dave watches the guy disappear into the dim light. Or rather, *hears* him. So, this is Missouri, he thinks, and chuckles to himself. He beelines to the café, pulls out his phone, gets a signal and taps in *CicadaMania*. Forget baseball. It seems he's in the heart of a rare thirteen-year cicada emergence. Since yesterday the nymphs—he liked that: *the nymphs*—have been waking up from their long sleep underground and marching into adulthood with a vengeance. Thousands of them. Probably millions. The Twittersphere's twitching with excitement: "We need cicada emojis!" "Good Magicicada morning!" "Get out there, folks, while the magic bugs sing!"

He crunches his way back into the park, full of adrenaline, stepping through piles of cicada casings. It takes skill not to crush the odd live one underfoot. The scale of the thing is amazing: he's a giant among insect Lilliputians, tracking them as they stream in the hundreds up an oak to join other bugs in various stages of molting. He uses his keychain LED light to look at one close up as it squeezes head-first out of its old husk like a diver shedding his wetsuit, only more graceful. With his cellphone he makes a shaky video, zooming in on the two huge, jade-red eyes. The cicada pops out vertically from its old brown skin with a set of tiny wings still origamied into its body. Gradually the wings unfold, pliable and gummy, making Dave think of the see-through rice paper on spring rolls. There's a lemon-yellow line running along the bug's wing edge. Ugly and beautiful at the same time.

Dave continues in the direction of the cicada guy, straight into the heart of the din. The racket's almost unbearable. Cicadas in every oak, on every inch of trunk, on every leaf, pouring out their shrill mating sound in the dawn. He wonders how the heck this racket works. Is it a general group announcement akin to "Hey, it's year thirteen. We're available!" Or is each individual bug clamouring for the attention of some other individual bug of the opposite persuasion and trying to drown out all the others? He stands in the midst of it, looks up through his cellphone camera, zooming in, zooming out, imagining he's a mad scientist on the brink of insanity, grinning. Never in his life has he grinned like that before.

He walks deeper into the woods, feels as if he's recklessly inhabiting himself, in awe of the bugs' driving instinct. What's their cue to change? Temperature? Moisture? Humidity? What's the prime number year that draws them out of the ground? If he divides the sound, he thinks he can hear different patterns, distinct songs, a beated precision, but moments after one appears it falls back into the whirring fray.

The sun shows above the horizon. The young cicada enthusiast suddenly appears next to him again, puts his hand on Dave's shoulder and shouts in his ear over the cacophony. "Isn't it great? It's a rock concert! Like when you slam your body against the loudspeaker to, you know, *feel* the music. Let it take you over." Dave nods. The guy's breath smells like minty hot chocolate. Above, the cicadas call "Pharaaaaoooh! Pharaaaaoooh!" The noise becomes the thrumming of his own nervous system, like he's had too much coffee. He tries to tune into the patterns to find some kind of order, but it's hopelessly unpredictable. Instead, he lets the chaos wash over him.

A cicada smashes into his cheek, like those accidental awkward stranger moments you have in long crowded corridors. Others fall from the trees onto his shoulders and back. He raises his head to the forest canopy to listen to the bugs vibrating their bodies in unison. When he turns to say something, the cicada guy has disappeared.

"One million of these guys per square acre right now in Missouri. One million," says an older man with a Fu Manchu moustache, crunching up to Dave, wearing a "Sing Fly Mate Die" T-shirt. "One million guys and one heckuva love song." He extends a meaty hand. "Name's Jackson." His eyes are a golden amber colour, like a fox.

Looking into the stranger's eyes, Dave answers. "Dunn... uh, Davidson."

The Fu Manchu man shakes Dave's hand a few seconds more than normal.

⌐

Dave enjoyed his spa weekend. Slept like a baby, no pills. He had a new appreciation for exfoliation. And to his surprise, Jackson was a wine aficionado.

He flew back home, the call of cicadas still coursing through his body. He joined CicadaWatch and changed his name to Dunn Davidson. A week later a package arrived in the mail containing a "Sing Fly Mate Die" T-shirt in his size. On his coffee table, taking pride of place, was a scaled-up model of a male *Magicicada tredecim*. Thirteen-year cicada, Brood Nineteen. They'd be back in 2024, but he'd be back in St. Louis before then.

The Watcher and the Watched

I collected all the cellphone shots. I *hand made* pillow replicas of all the penises. *Hand*-painted, *hand*-dyed silk! It took me freakin' months. I embroidered the nicknames on each one of them and filled a whole gallery room. People took their shoes off and romped around with the penis pillows. Women loved it, took selfies with their favourites. Most guys seemed repelled by the replica members of their brethren and just stood around with their arms crossed. There was a soundtrack, looping voices reading text messages from the guys, in all their unintentional crudeness and sweetness. "I'm kinda lonely but not totally lonely," "Babe, I'm ready when you are," "You're just a bitch with a hate-on for men," and my all-time favourite, "I would please like to marry you if you are real virgin." Sorry, dude. One guy recognized his wang in the promo shots and threatened to sue me. No case. Plus, do you want to advertise that your thing has a birthmark that looks like a worm? I don't think so.

I have Walen to thank for getting me to all this, even if it meant we had to break up. He was not right for me anyway, uni teaching assistant, obsessing about his stupid thesis all the time. Like, who does their thesis on fireflies? It sounds romantic, but believe me, it isn't. I was in love with him, but not his meh ideas. Like the lecture he invited me to. "The *Photuris* female blah blah preys on the male of another species blah blah so she gets his protective chemicals blah blah blah." I wanted to poke my eyes out within, like, one minute. But then I had an idea: Fireflies, the Triumph of Nostalgia over Reality. My first art installation. For once, Walen got excited about something I did. "Tracy, you can have my *Photuris* stock. I have way too many and the study's over now. As long as you set them free afterwards." Of course I would set them free.

I had to keep the larvae on damp paper towels so they'd hatch. When the adults popped out, I stuck them in mason jars in the basement. It was like a distant galaxy in there, all winking stars in the darkness, the males flippin' their signals for the ladies, on-on-off, on-off-off-on, horny Morse code of bioluminescence. The show, well. Someone mentioned the word "inhumane," and I was, like, "Really? They're bugs."

Later I realized I didn't need live ones. When it all went bad and the gallery floor was littered with thousands of dried-up fireflies, I just renamed the installation "The Triumph of Reality over Nostalgia" and broke up with Walen. I rewrote my artist's statement. In third person to give it that air of critic's authority:

"McAffey explores the gap between human intervention in the natural world and the non-linear, non-narrative space of memory and yearning."

So basically, in our quest to illuminate the whole damn planet we've pushed our glowing friends to *lights out*. Art fans love the eco-shit.

Speaking of which, I started dating this guy, well, virtually, called digitaldegas. He was full of shit half the time, but then he'd just say things that would rip my heart, like, "People secretly want the worst truth not the better lie." Or "Heidegger and Sartre were just pretentious gits, theorizing out of their buttholes about existence." He sent me a picture of his dick, which didn't really turn me on. But he was a freakin' networking genius and as long as I kept stroking his ego the publicity hype flowed. Bloggers started contacting me for web interviews. Thank you, little exoskeletons. Two years out of art school and life was looking good.

But then it went to the next level. Some asshole legitimate critic got wind of me through digitaldegas and came out swinging, saying I had no imagination and I quote: *The result is a dubious concoction of contrived juvenilia.* Well, la-dee-fucking-dah. I swear the guy hated women. I dumped digitaldegas. Thing is, I actually had zero ideas now that art-fucks were scrutinizing me. The only thing I could think of was copying myself à la Ai Weiwei and redoing the Triumph of Reality with a different spin. But that was lame. I was done with the bugs. What I really wanted to do was ratchet up the social relevance and provoke people. That's what art's for, right?

I still had zero ideas so I pissed away my days on Facebook and hookup sites, or Snapchat. A couple of guys sent me dick-shots that were more interesting than their faces. So I started a file folder and just started shoving the pics in there. Then I got this idea. First I asked guys to describe themselves in five words or less. This was pretty interesting already. "Goldenboy. Ripped. Your beautiful," for example, was poetic in a guy-haiku-bad-grammar kinda way. So then after some texting, sexting and other chat I would ask for a dick-shot. If they did it I figured it was consent. This got even more interesting. "Titan," for example, was anything but. Some guys used pretty cool Instagram filters. And there's no coincidence that Mr. Gaming-Is-My-Life's pic was bathed in the blue light of a monitor.

My friend Bree said it was unethical. Ethical, my ass! This was the twenty-first century! She said if a *guy* did this they would nail him for being sexist, so it's just reverse sexism. Which is exactly my point. Why can't girls have a little fun, too? Trust your public with irony, I say.

One guy refused to send me a photo. The one guy I was actually interested in—Dev. He kept saying, "Come on, talk to me, talk to *me*, not my dick." I kept asking him, but only in between some chatting about living in the city versus the country and where you go when you die. I started thinking about him way too much, but in a good way. But he still wouldn't be part of my project.

⁓

Walen came to the penis pillow show. Not that his was there. Within two seconds of saying "hi," he announced he'd just been to the dentist, as if this proved he was a whole different person and had moved on. He showed me his new crown. His breath was minty. Our pheromones didn't talk to each other, and that was that. I could tell that the only person who'd been in his mouth recently was a dentist. When he walked away I felt something that was similar to love, I think. Well, love that was lost and hobbling into the dark woods.

Dev and I kept up—only on email. He said texting was not what opposable thumbs were made for. He bugged me about why I was doing such a—as he put it—"lightweight" show. "All you did was take an IKEA ball room, fill it with adults instead of kids and add sex." I argued with him about how I saw it as "politicizing the penis" and making it an object of fun and manipulation, but he wouldn't buy it. He smelled fear, he said. And loathing. And longing.

"You think you're all wild-ass and free-form, but your chaos is a cover. It's anxiety dressed up like the king's fool. You're careful not to reveal anything about yourself, yet you ask others to do that very thing." I wrote back, "So hate me. I don't care." He answered, "Don't hate me, Tracy. Hate what I say." We both went offline.

A couple of weeks later, Dev emailed a photo. A caribou running down a deserted highway in what looked like maybe the Yukon, or Finland, I don't know. It really got me. That lonely stretch of road, turning a corner to somewhere. Or nowhere? The caribou looked spooked, like it was trying to outrun something, maybe a logging truck or some predator, although I don't think caribou *have* any predators.

Wolves? It looked like a place I'd like to go to, but not alone. All those icy mountains and stunted boreal trees. I made it my screen saver so I could look at it all the time. Sometimes I got up at night and stared at it. What did Dev mean by, "You never know what people are until you see them. And even then you might be blind"? At one point, I thought the caribou was farther down the road, but it wasn't. Was there a shadow just appearing in the left side of the photo? I sent Dev a text asking him if he took the photo himself. No answer. Where the photo was taken. No answer. Where do you live? He typed back, "In your mind" and fell off the radar.

Life started to suck. I started poking a pin into my fingers just so I could feel something. Anything. Little red blood beads all in a row. Fireflies do it. Reflex bleeding. Makes bitter blood. I wanted to know where Dev was. I wanted to see that place in the photo. I wanted to *be* the caribou. So I went north to the boreal forest.

Art Review Canada. *Breathing the Beast*. By Cynthia Chatman.
    Due North Gallery's new show, "The Watcher and the Watched," by Tracy McAffey, has caused quite a stir. Normally, McAffey shows in Regina, but this time, the opening for her newest installation is in Whitehorse, Yukon. And it's a radical departure for McAffey, who up until now has designed installations that tweak people's emotions, toy with gender bias, or are satirical and playful, like the popular "I Would Please Like to Marry You," with its myriad penis pillows and looping messages from hookup sites. With her prior work, McAffey always remained behind the scenes. But in "The Watcher and the Watched," the artist is present and not only gives us a glimpse of her vulnerability, she explores the intersection of human and

animal consciousness, and how our bodies might shape our very psyche.

The public enters the gallery into an open space with log benches facing a large screen. McAffey enters wearing a flesh-coloured bodysuit. She holds up a handwritten sign that reads, "Please do not touch the artist during this performance." Then she sits, facing the audience, in front of a mirror and methodically applies makeup to create the face of a female boreal woodland caribou. Her face gets a neutral greasepaint base layer, then on top, a brushed-on layer of brown. She attaches long, black, fake ungulate eyelashes and smudges charcoal black all the way around her eyes and on the lids. She then puts on a custom caribou head (that has short antlers like twigs from a tree) and steps into a hand-stitched caribou hide quadsuit with her legs operating as the back feet and her arms—extended by short stilts—as the front. McAffey's co-creator, fabric artist Janine Lowry, who is well-known for her eerie taxidermied animal skin—human bust hybrids, built the authentic quadsuit and head that McAffey wears. While the artist is assembling herself, a small herd appears on the screen behind her, grazing peacefully. When finished, the transformed McAffey, with her wide tufted hooves and tawny caribou head and body, seems to join them. She walks amongst the audience, stops on occasion, and looks into people's eyes for extended periods. This is quite moving, sometimes surprising. Some people giggle, others are sad or serious, as is McAffey. When it comes to my turn, I find it unsettling. Am I regarding an animal or a person? What do animals seek in our eyes that humans don't? On this day there is a startling interaction between McAffey and a male audience member in a wheelchair who—contrary to the stated rules—reaches out with one fingertip and tenderly caresses her ears and neck, causing the artist to cry. They seem to forge a very strong connection, or perhaps they know each other. There is always risk in a show with audience participation. But being less in control of her work has created for the artist something more spontaneous that reaches deeper than her other work. Once this unscripted moment is over, there is what sounds like brief gunshots or a sudden burst of stampeding hooves. McAffey returns to the front and starts running in slow motion in place on a treadmill. At first she's running with the herd on the screen behind her. But her herd disperses and disappears offscreen, leaving her alone. Is there a pursuer? She looks behind her occasionally and starts removing parts of the costume in flight. First the hand stilts, so she is now upright. Next the hoofed back legs come off. The head is removed last. She stops running. Back to her beige bodysuit, she begins smearing off her makeup, then looks one last time over her shoulder. At which point, the lights abruptly go out. When they come back on, there is neither human nor animal. McAffey is gone.

Knedlíky

Iris stands in the airport arrivals hall, her new suitcase heavy in her right hand. The crowds have thinned out. Incomprehensible announcements from the public address system ricochet off the walls. She scans the waiting area for his face. Twenty minutes later the hall is empty. Petr doesn't answer her calls. Fed up with waiting, she takes a taxi into Prague. The taxi driver is friendly and speaks good English, urges her to sit in the front seat the better to see the sights of "the jewel of Czechia," as he calls it, patting her on the left shoulder. It is an unusually hot day in the middle of August. Her thighs stick to the seat. He asks her if she's travelling alone and she answers yes, but she's meeting somebody. Should have said "a man." They pass over the Vltava. Amorous couples float in rented paddleboats shaped like Cadillacs. Others go for the more clichéd white swan.

"It is so romantic, no?" He puts his right hand on her thigh, his fingertips sticky like the pads of frogs' feet. Why does she always attract these types? She puts up with it stiffly. She's not one of those women who can retaliate with a resounding slap. The rest of the ride is awkward. And she has the impression he's taking her on a roundabout route. She always studies a city map before her arrival anywhere.

Her exotic travels make her seem exciting to friends, but deep down she knows she's brown-paper ordinary. She never mentions the men she meets online. Her criteria for suitability. This is one compartment of her life, or perhaps one of several, that remains locked. It is her privilege, she believes, to choose what she does and does not reveal about herself. Ultimately, her goal is a love match, but so far it hasn't worked out that way. Had her colleagues known, for example, that she'd had dalliances with a Peruvian rancher that resulted in an STD, it could have compromised her professional reputation. And, anyway, it is her nature to withhold.

The spires of Prague's medieval castle loom into view. The taxi driver finally lifts his hand off her thigh and points out a stone arch at the end of a cobbled street. "Apartments Praha," he announces, patting her shoulder for the last time. She slithers out humiliated, angry that she hadn't slapped him.

Because she doesn't really know Petr yet, just to be safe, she's rented a flat outside the historic downtown. After meeting the owner, she lugs her too-big suitcase up three flights of stairs and wrestles with the strange door lock and equally mystifying antique key. Once inside the capacious apartment, with its period carved doors, antique light fixtures and burnished wood flooring, she flops onto the bed. Staring up at the high-coved ceilings, she starts to think maybe it's crazy to come all this way to meet a man she's found on the Internet, someone she's had pretty amazing Skype sex with. But it's too late now to have doubts. Petr's the best—well, the only—cyber-lover she's ever had, and he's a famous chef with his own TV show. His flair for cooking reaches into the realms of food porn. Erotic in every way—at least virtually. At his suggestion she'd bought an Us-Vibe Pro with the partner app, which really amped up the action, and a racy negligee he chose online, which, amazingly, came in plus sizes. Skype eliminated all her inhibitions.

After twelve hours in the black hole of jet lag, she wakes at noon the next day. Petr has left a long-winded apology on her cellphone, inviting her to come by the restaurant for dinner.

⁓

Seven p.m. she gets on the tram to Vinohrady. It's jammed with sweaty tourists and grumpy locals. A tall, broad-shouldered man in a rumpled grey blazer stands and graciously offers her his seat with a theatrical sweep of his hand. Chivalry is not dead. He holds his large black case aloft so she can squeeze through.

Petr's two-Michelin-star restaurant is on a bumpy brick side street in the heart of Vinohrady. She enters. From the back of the room Petr manhandles a waitress as he bustles toward her. His eyes linger on Iris's hips for a brief second, as if they might be larger than he expected. He's shorter than his Skype self suggests. A lot shorter. His head reaches just below her eyes so she has to curtsy to kiss him, as if he's a midget king. A surprisingly chaste kiss. Other than that, he still ticks off all her boxes for ideal man—handsome, professional, financially secure, foreign.

The restaurant is decorated in an austere modern style, like a trendy dentist's office. Petr does not introduce her to anyone on his staff. Taking her by the hand, he leads, well, pulls her to a romantic table in the corner.

His cellphone rings.

"Just a second. I have to take this…. Yes, yes, *beruško*, I will. Okay, next Thursday," he says in a placating voice. Continuing to talk on the phone, he uses his free hand to pull out a chair for Iris. She sits while he talks.

Once he's finished the call, he joins her at the table and snaps his fingers for the waitress to bring the menu board. He reads it out loud. "Tonight: *wild boar in hibiscus sauce, root vegetable confit, silky knedlíky dumplings with pork cracklings and kefir dressing.* This is music, this

food! It sings. Or if you prefer, the Dégustation Menu of seven courses, but this takes very long." He glances at his expensive watch.

When the entrée arrives, he reaches over to slice the meat for her.

"*Wild boar*. They're taking over the countryside in Česko.
Overbreeding like lice and eating the maize, trampling everything.
Government has made their hunting season all year now. This is good
for us. Ours is best wild boar available. Taste." He thrusts the fork at
her mouth.

She chews and nods her approval. It seems, actually, a little under-
done for her taste.

He points at the dumplings. "*Knedlíky*. Potato dumplings, this—
this!—is nouvelle Bohemian. Not peasant food, the old traditional
dumplings, too greasy and served with bad meat. These are *gastro-
nomic* knedlíky. The dough, it must rest for hours before you make
them; this way, the dumplings are light and soft, like a pillow for the
tiniest mouse."

The maître d' comes and whispers in Petr's ear.

"I must go for a moment. I will be back, Iris." She sits alone with
the flickering candle and the paisley wallpaper. *The tiniest mouse.* She
feels underdressed.

The food is exquisite. But Petr doesn't really eat. He just moves the
food around on his plate as if reading omens in a clump of entrails.
Mostly, he drinks and pours wine.

"You have tried the *pigéage*, the grapes-crushing with bare feet?" he
asks, his pitch rising.

"No—"

"It is incredible, so sensual. Especially the red. And all the people
having fun together trampling in that squishy mess. Incredible." He
clinks her glass a little too enthusiastically.

Afterwards they sneak off to his place for non-cyber sex. The apartment looks hardly lived in, frozen in some previous decade, a time
capsule isolated from the rest of his life as the innovator of the "new

Czech cuisine." On the side table is a video titled *I Have a Crush on You*, showing a woman in lacy shorts wearing a pair of blue leather stilettos. She chooses not to comment on it. Petr excuses himself for a moment and quickly goes into the bedroom. There is the sound of a drawer being opened and closed. He re-emerges, smiling.

They start off awkwardly in the living room, like human bumper cars, their bodies not entirely translated to the less familiar third dimension. At this point the ease of their former Skype foreplay is not evident. His torso is shorter. Her arms are longer. He removes her sandals, momentarily admires them, and caresses her size-eleven feet, assuring her they are the loveliest he's ever seen.

"You wouldn't say that if you had to buy shoes for them," she answers. He wants her to step with her bare feet on his chest—or did he say stomp?—which she does half-heartedly and without her full weight, one foot at a time, worried about breaking something. Still, it's obvious he finds it exciting. He pulls her into the bedroom. Semi-attached, they tumble onto the bed. When her head hits the pillow, she thinks back to his comment in the restaurant: *that squishy mess.* Petr draws his fingertips slowly across her skin as she stares out at the bedroom, which seems oddly feminine—floral wallpaper, fussy valance. There's a white oval mirror which captures only the upper half of their bodies, as if they've been sawn in half by a magician.

"Who is 'Beruško'?" she asks out of the blue just as Petr is about to unbutton her blouse.

"It is 'darling' or 'sweetheart.'"

"But what does it mean?"

"It means actually 'a type of little beetle.'"

"Beetle? That's weird."

"No, Iris. It is a way of endearment in Czech."

He unwraps her. This is how it feels, like someone meticulously opening a hot filo pastry. He touches her face. She finds it subtly nauseating. The receptors on her skin hint at some fundamental error.

At first she ignores the sensation, thinking it's nerves. He continues running his fingers down from her collarbone, to her breasts, her navel, stopping and lingering at her ankles, tracing around the bones, fondling each toe, while whispering words in Czech she can't understand. A clock ticks too loudly from the bedside table as if suppressing its alarm. A small kernel of resistance grows in her gut.

Grilled duck breast on porcini risotto, smoked beef tongue with yellow pea and apple.... Their gourmet romance and ungraceful couplings continue for the next few days. No more stomping. He's a good, if showoff, chef. But he makes love as if each movement is a step in a recipe he already knows. Or as if her body is someone else's. As if he's holding something back. She fakes it anyway, chewing her fists to distract herself, which she is sure he mistakes for unbridled passion. Several times she catches him glance furtively at his cellphone, and he often stares beyond her to the same spot on the dresser where there's a short outline of dust. After a week it feels like a routine.

"Beruško," Petr lies back on the bed. "You seemed so large and strong on the Skype. So strong you could crush me like an ant. Could you be like that again? I bought you something." He reaches under the bed and lifts out a box containing a pair of red ladies' shoes. Size eleven. Very observant. Very expensive high heels, and very pointy. They don't call them "stiletto" for nothing. She pictures silent criminals slicing into the hearts of their victims.

"Try them, Iris."

She forces them on like one of the ugly stepsisters.

"Ah, they are perfect! I feel helpless and pitiful just looking at you." He lies down on the carpet beside her.

"Oh, please, mistress. Don't step on me, don't crush me to bits," he wheedles, clearly aroused. She teeters over him feeling both powerful and idiotic, hovering on the border of fetish and ordinary desire. What ensues she will never be proud of, but she admits to herself that "crushing" him has released her forever from the illusion that love can be found in a list of ideal criteria.

It's a relief to board the tram back to her flat. And there, seated midway at a window seat on the left, is the man in the crumpled grey blazer. Not handsome, she notes, but... notable. She sits behind him. Although his back is turned, she has the distinct impression he can see her. At one point his oversized head bobs just a little, as if he's listening to music. But he doesn't have headphones on. There's a reddish splotch on the back of his neck that looks like the outline of a country. She likes it. She wants to touch it. He gets off one stop before hers, a plain and unremarkable man who probably lives in a plain and unremarkable flat. She pictures him in his kitchen, hunched over the table eating plain-old greasy downscale Czech dumplings. Licking his big fingers. He seems to glide instead of walk out of the lamplight and into the dark.

Back in her flat, she lies on the couch, pinching her stomach fat. She switches on *Titanic* (the only DVD) dubbed in Czech. At the part where Rose says, "Put your hands on me, Jack," the dubbing is out of sync with her lips.

"*Beruško*, I need to tell you something. I'm so glad you are here." Neither of them has had the guts to end the relationship yet. Petr sits her down on the bed. She tries to ignore the fact that he called her a beetle.

"This morning I find out that I lose one Michelin star." Tears make his eyes glossy. She remembers their first day together, how she had watched him commanding his staff in the restaurant, how she had felt the scope of his ambition and wondered how she could carve out a space in his life. She had thought, stupidly, that the cybersex would be a prelude to a real sexual life, a romantic life. She wanted to be cherished, not an object of someone's sick fantasy. His head is turned away from her. In profile, he looks like a different person, someone she doesn't know, the tiny crush freak that he is. The two of them sit on his bed as the sun withdraws. His cellphone rings. He holds up his index finger to pause their conversation.

"*Sakra*, Thomas! I tell you put order through two days ago. Call Miloš and get him in to prep. I don't care he has a day off...."

"Sorry." Petr sits back down on the bed. He makes a tense spidery shape in the bedspread with his hand. Without looking her in the eye he tells her that he'll be out of town for a few days for a Culinary World Cup Challenge in Riga. He doesn't invite her, but she's secretly glad. His departure is an easy way for them to admit that their non-virtual relationship is a failure. But she's keeping the shoes.

She takes a different tram back to her flat. The man in the grey blazer is on that one, too, sitting in front, with a black guitar case at his feet. There are stickers all over it: *Just follow your Soul*; *Scuse me while I kiss the sky*. She wonders in which direction he lives—coming or going. Ten minutes into the ride, he comes down the aisle toward her. As he makes his way he hands a small leaflet to each passenger.

"Tiki Palač Praha," he says to her, a phrase she doesn't understand. He extends the paper and adds in English, "You must come. Soul. It is for everyone," his voice inflecting in a singsong way. Startled, she takes it. He smiles—a smile you could step inside, it's so wide and inviting. She assumes the leaflet is for a religious event, folds it and politely puts it in her purse without looking further at it. He gets off at a different stop than last time.

Back at the flat she switches on *Titanic* again and manages to change it back to the English track so people's mouths match their speech. It

makes the sentimentality more glaring. When Jack clings like a persistent cliché to debris in the cold sea and assures Rose, "You're going
to die an old lady, warm in her bed," Iris decides it would be better to
die young in a sinking ship.

"Call me if a green fairy shows up." The server winks, placing the glass
of absinthe in front of her. She had decided, after uncharacteristically
tossing her itinerary and randomly walking the Malá Strana all day,
to go back in the early evening to one of the hole-in-the-wall bars in
Staré Město that Petr had shown her. A cozy corner with a view of
the street and a glass of absinthe to celebrate Petr's *ab-sence*—her little
joke to herself. Most of the patrons speak in Czech, a language that
sounds to her like someone sawing a dry piece of firewood. Opposite
her sits a scrawny British woman who reminds her of her mother.
The same frantic knitting-needle hands. Diffident servers bustle ef-
ficiently in their black cinched vests, transporting uneaten food back
to the bar's inner recesses. To her right, Aussies knock back flights
of Pilsner and eat what look like those "peasant" sausages Petr had
ranted about. She still had hope then, as he'd pulled her by the hand
through an unmarked door set in a white wall and led her to the pal-
ace with ornate fountains, statues and a very odd wall of artificial
limestone like something out of a malarial dream. Now all she has is
the shoes. Which she is wearing. They are very red.

She stares at an old 1920s theatre poster—*"Ze života hmyzu,* The
Insect Play, by Karel and Josef Capek." Below the title, a hump-backed
man in a leather jacket rolls a large dung ball, which seems a perfect
summation of her exploits. *Travelling for love. Bunch of crap.* I'll drink
to that, she thinks, and does, several times—*na zdraví, na zdraví.*

When she reaches into her purse to pay the tab, she sees the leaflet from yesterday and unfolds it. *Thursday.* "Slávek and the Soul

Brothers Live in Concert," it says in English. So not a religious event. Music. It starts at seven-thirty. What the hell. She has nothing better to do. She can't pronounce the venue name with its collision of consonants, so she points to it and asks the waiter where it is. His eyebrows shoot up, but he scribbles the route on a napkin for her and she runs in her killer shoes to get a taxi.

Tikki Palác Praha is a tiny venue in Žižkov, with a turquoise painted exterior and an entrance flanked by two trumpet-blowing stone monkeys. Inside, it's teeming with kitsch. Glass pineapple light fixtures festoon the ceiling, tribal masks leer from the walls, and everyone is clutching a tropical drink. She pays the ten euro cover charge, and the Hawaiian-shirted doorman with nose piercings points over the crowd. The only seat left is directly in front of the band. She squeezes past the crowded tables and plants herself in a sea-green chair. Her complimentary mai tai arrives on a tray held by a grass-skirted hunk. The house goes dark for the show to begin.

A man leaps in front of a vintage microphone and shouts, "Ladies and gentlemen! Slávek and the Soul Brothers!" And strolling onstage is none other than her man from the tram, electric guitar slung over his shoulder. He's in a black button-up shirt with a piano keys tie, black high-back trousers, black and white wingtip shoes, and his hair is slicked back. He cues the band, leans into the mic and launches into a deep-voiced version of "Feeling Good." He looks down at Iris and sings the first line, "Birds flying high, you know how I feel..." and she thinks her body's going to explode. She orders another drink called "Death by Volcano" and sucks the drink down to the lava-red bottom while the band plays "Super Freak" and "Shotgun." Anywhere there's room, people are dancing. A woman in a webby black dress grabs Iris's hand to join them. Which Iris does, even though she doesn't dance. Especially in high heels. At the end of the set, Slávek sings a heart-shredding ballad in Czech which lights up her entire nervous system.

Afterwards the band gathers around a table and eats in a cloud of cigarette smoke. She teeters over to tell them how much she enjoyed the music. She stands awkwardly by the table, waiting for an opportunity to speak.

"You are woman from the tram. Come. Come and sit down." He grabs a chair from behind and swings it over to their table. "I am Slávek. Of course, you know that."

"Iris." More plates of food arrive at the table. Slávek introduces her to each band member, pointing with his bear-paw hand. He turns back to her, looks down at the screaming red shoes, and does a silent wolf whistle. She winks back.

"You are from where, Iris? US?"

"No, Canada!" she says with flourish, surprising herself.

"Iris from Canada, you must try this! Traditional Czech knedlíky with fried Spam. Praha-Pacific fusion food."

"Are you kidding?" she answers.

"No, really. It is good. The comfort food of Hawaiians and Pražáks. Trust me. But first you must learn to say *kned-lí-ky*."

"Ka-led-nickie?" The band bursts into laughter. She's terrible at languages. Especially after four drinks.

"Say again. *Kned-lí-ky*...." Slávek's face lights up comically; his large hand holds the fork aloft. She can't say it because she can't stop laughing. The fork hovers in front of her, a small morsel of glistening dough captured on its tines.

"Okay, okay. Kuh-ned-lee-kee."

"Brava, Iris. Now you are official *knedlíkový*: lover of dumplings."

She leans toward him, opens her mouth, and lets Slávek slide the fork between her lips.

Our Invisible Friend

Barton. They knew the guy for over ten years, but he doesn't appear in a single photo. How? Well, for one, he was the photographer. No one ever thought of snatching the camera and taking a shot with him in it. Why would they? The thing was a black, intimidating piece of serious technology. Even if they'd asked, he wouldn't have let them touch it. This was way before everyone had an iPhone. His darkroom troglodyte existence was a mystery to them. It never occurred to anyone that he'd be developing *other* photos that weren't of the gang doing Jägermeister shooters, the guys hungover in their underwear, and Carly making killer Cheez Whiz and jalapeño nachos in the famous purple bachelor basement suite they always managed to cram into.

"Oh god, look at this one." Sandra passed around a poster-sized shot of a bratty-looking girl in profile seated on a crushed velvet cushion wailing on a saxophone. "He calls it, 'Little Boy Blue.'" On the wall behind the girl was the famous Coltrane album cover, *A Love Supreme*. Next to her was a taxidermied stork. There were square chunks of shattered safety glass scattered at her feet. It was brilliant. Clearly, he was a fan of the great jazz photographer William Gottlieb.

Garth cracked a beer and scooped the photo off the table. "Geezuz Murphy, could this really be by our buddy?"

Carly carried in a huge plate of nachos from her kitchen and put them on the coffee table. Everyone eyed the orangey stack queasily.

Sandra leaned into Garth and took the photo from him. "Her hair and the way she's posing look exactly like that Waléry photo of Josephine Baker."

"Says the art history major."

"Shut up, Craig."

"Actually, she looks a bit like you, Sandra. Barton had a crush on you, you know." Sandra evil-eyed Craig.

"I just can't reconcile this guy with the big-nosed, flat-footed schlub we knew as Barton."

"I know."

"He didn't have a big nose," Jenny finally spoke up, distractedly twirling her hair around her fingers.

Garth asked, "What about the, uh, skirt thingy, the slip? The way it's just showing her, uh, panties. It's, you know, sort of...."

"Risqué?" Sandra answered.

Carly shrieked, "Po-orn?"

"Yeah."

Sandra took another look, "Well, if it is, then it's really good porn. Personally, I don't think it's provocative."

The nachos were untouched. No one really ate nachos anymore.

"But who are all these kids? I don't remember any of them hanging out with him, ever."

"Probably, like, relatives or neighbours? Barton was a good guy. A sweet guy." They needed Carly to keep asserting the goodness in life, to spread the fairy dust every so often.

"He wasn't fond of kids," Sandra said. "He didn't hate them, but he couldn't relate to them at all. He disliked their underdeveloped minds."

"What?" Garth plunked his glass on the table. "How do you know that?"

"He told me once."

Craig gestured with his wineglass. "I think they're bloody genius. But I think a few of them could be deemed borderline porn, or at least 'suggestive' by today's standards. Did the kids' parents know he was taking these shots?"

"No, no. This can't be Bart," Carly said. "I'm so confused. I just thought Bart was Bart." She got up and passed the nachos around.

Jenny, always the peacemaker, carefully pulled a congealed hunk of cheese off the top of the chips. It looked like a giant scab. "We should do a gallery show. We owe it to him. We're his only family now. We don't have to use his name. These kids are all grown up now. The photos are... they're amazing."

"Right. We'd have to leave out the borderline ones," Sandra said. "Personally, I always thought he had some hidden talent. There was just something about him."

They all started hacking away at the nachos.

Jenny peeled off another cheesy blob. "I didn't know he knew about jazz. I mean, no one listened to jazz in the 90s. It was so dead then, right Garth?"

"Dave Douglas, *Constellations*."

"Shut up, Craig."

"I thought his tastes ran more to rock. The only song he could play on his guitar was Guns N' Roses' 'November Rain.'"

"Wrong, Garth. It was 'Tender Surrender.'"

"Fuck. This is awful."

"I know. Poor Barton."

"No, the nachos."

⌒

At their next get-together, they laid out all seventeen photos on Jenny's white living room carpet.

"This is everything from the locker. Is there some kind of order?

They're not dated. Is there a *message*, like, why he committed suicide?" Jenny asked, sitting down beside Garth.

"Hey hey hey, we don't know for sure if it was suicide."

"But who goes hiking at dusk in Capilano Canyon?"

"Barton," Garth, Sandra and Carly all said at the same time.

"Let's not get ahead of ourselves here. Let's just figure out what his overall theme is, was, if any. What's he trying to say?" Craig, the logic wrangler. He stood up and surveyed the photos on view. "I see a couple of jazz references. See that one with the little skinny black kid in the fez? Holding a huge jailer's-sized fob of *keys*? It's all about Thelonious Monk. King of the cluster chord. The right wrong note." No one deigned to challenge the man once referred to as the Child Savant.

"That would explain the cloistery ceiling."

Sandra was scrutinizing the photo. "His sense of lighting is phenomenal. The outfit's kind of Van Gogh-ish, like the painting of the Zoave guy with the cochlear red fez. But why?"

Craig laughed his haughty laugh. "*Cochineal*. The cochlear's an auditory nerve. *Cochineal's* the red bug. I doubt Barton was on that level of arty-farty references. He was more a *Mad Magazine* kinda guy."

"Naw, I never thought of him as ironic. He was a straight-up humour man."

"No, that's *you*, Garth."

"Geezuz, who was this guy? Barton. Were we mean to him?" Jenny said.

"No. We just kind of ignored him. He was our group mascot."

"Mascot. Geezuz, Carly."

"Hey Jen, is Jack coming today?"

"Should be, any minute."

"I haven't seen him for ages."

Craig butted in, "He's about the same, only with ten ex-girlfriends, a new dog and one less testicle."

"Oversharing!"

"So." Garth intervened, placing a box on the coffee table. "Like I told you guys, there was this box of letters, between Barton and a guy named *Serge*."

"Oh–they could have been lovers!"

Craig blasted out a startling, "Ha!"

Garth ignored Craig. "Not necessarily, Carly. They could have been just friends or photography buffs swapping ideas. I've read all of these. Most of them are pretty boring. No hint of a romance. In the last one from 1998, Barton says, 'Send your stuff to me.' Plus, 'I will send you the shots I did in New Orleans.' Then there's a bunch of details about lenses, which I will spare you. There's no last name for this Serge or address because Bart only saved the letters, not the envelopes."

"Barton and New Orleans is just *wrong*. I'm sorry, guys, but it sounds like Eeyore goes to Paris or something," said Jenny.

Craig sat smugly with his arms crossed.

"Well, I happen to know he had relatives in Texas," Sandra said.

"He did?"

"Yup," Sandra nodded.

"Sandra, how is it that you seem to have secret knowledge of our invisible friend?" Craig asked.

"It's not secret. Unlike some of you, I actually sometimes took the time to talk to him. He wasn't the schlub you all make him out to be."

"Maybe he shot all of these in New Orleans in someone's studio," Jenny offered quietly. No one responded.

The doorbell rang. Jack strode in carrying a six-pack of beer. "Guys, I have more news. You know that sealed envelope in the locker? Barton wasn't Barton. He was freakin' Pascal."

"Oh, for heaven's sake!" Jenny poured more wine for everybody except Jack, starting with Garth first, of course. Now that she had sloughed off her husband, certain old alliances were reasserting themselves.

"He changed his name in 1987. Before we knew him, he was Pascal Aucoin." He said the name with mock French flair.

"Oh my god," Carly perked up. "Maybe he was in the witness protection program!"

"Nope. He was adopted. Young."

"This could explain New Orleans," said Garth.

Four days later they were all at Garth's perfectly tidy but outdated condo, staring at the photo montage titled "Ah Um a Song of Sixpence."

"This one is deeply weird. The pig looks human. Kind of collage. I'm starting to see how this fits in with our old buddy Barton."

"Creepy clowns always scare me. Creepy half-naked kid clowns are even worse."

"'Goodbye Porkpie Hat,'" said Craig.

"Huh?

"It's 'Goodbye Porkpie Hat.' Mingus album *Mingus Ah Um*.

"Oh, I get it. *Pork* pie, the pig."

"But where are the four and twenty blackbirds?" said Carly as Garth slid a coaster under her wineglass before it hit the glass tabletop. Jack put his beer down on the table before Garth could coasterize him.

"Craig, is it my imagination, or does the pig coming out of the pie look a tiny bit like you?"

"It's your imagination."

"It does!" Carly laughed. She got up close, like a surgeon reading an X-ray. "Is this some kind of, I don't know, mocking of us? A puzzle we're too stupid to solve, like a dumbed-down CSI?"

"Garth, what the fuck *is* this music?"

"Not yer grandmother's rock and roll."

"Are you kidding me? This is, like, some fuckwad loser's bedroom recording with bad speaker static."

"Indie group called The Megaphones. Barton would have liked it."

"I doubt it. Muzak for old hippies. He was an R.E.M. man." Jack downed the rest of his beer and went to pour another one.

Garth shot back, "Why are you still such a dick, Jack?"

From the kitchen, Jack flicked an old snapshot across the room to Carly. In the photo they were standing with their arms wrapped around each other.

"Wow. We both look so young! And look at you, so proud of your tiny campfire."

"The early beginnings of your serial conquests," said Craig.

"Was that the Tofino camping trip? Was Barton there?" Jenny sucked on the ends of her hair.

"Well, duh, there's photos."

"It's like he was always there but not there."

Craig leaned back and laid both arms across the top of the sofa. "By the way, he didn't take the shots in New Orleans, not when I was there."

"Of course, as the expert on Barton's secret life, you would know that."

"Yes, I would," Craig took his sweet time answering. "I was with him. In New Orleans. The city of gumbo and crazy Creoles. April 18, 1995."

"Whoring in the crawfish capital...."

"Hardly. I was in Austin for an engineering conference. We met in New Orleans for a couple of days. He didn't have his camera with him. It was in the shop back at home."

"But in the letter, he says...."

Carly was absorbed, singing along to the music, "I miss my dearest friend...."

"We ate alligator, drank a lot of weak piss beer. That's about all I remember. Except maybe the eccentric waiter named Xavier."

"Man, you will always remain a mystery to me. And I'd like to keep it that way."

Jenny sat cross-legged on the floor, running her hand across the carpet. "I'm not sure I should tell this, but once when he was wasted he said there was this 'door' he could never open."

"Door?"

"Like, some taboo thing. I assumed it was suicide, which, in the light of things, makes sense." She glanced up at Jack.

"Depression, most likely. The guy was fucking walking doom."

"Or it could be love for little girls?" Carly ventured.

A hush fell over everyone.

Craig spoke up. "For Christ's sake, people. It was the 1980s. He was a closet gay. Who gives a shit anyway these days. I just wish he was still around, even if nobody really got him."

"Yeah."

It rained the devil's pitchforks at the show's opening. Jack pulled up in his Mazda RX-7 with Jenny beside him. Garth was a no-show. Thirty-two people turned out, a good number of them from the Vancouver Photography Club. Carly cried. The club offered to buy seven of the photos for their archives. Apparently, they were that good. Sandra felt vindicated at her discovery of genius. But apparently the photos weren't actually by Barton. Halfway into the show, one of the club members verified definitively that they were by a well-known American photographer named Serge Thuriot.

"You know, I kinda liked this Barton better."

"Well, I like the old one."

Craig squinted into the rain. "I don't even know who the hell he is—was—anymore. But I'm claiming the Mingus photo."

Velvet Voice

"As soon as all of us were in one place we'd do a few gigs," she told me, dragging on a cigarette and nursing a wheatgrass smoothie. "We hardly ever practised; we just—" She blew out a perfect stream of smoke, then sipped the green drink—"winged it." Apparently, that was how Rick the lead guitarist, a.k.a. Rat Boy, liked it. Raw. Or, as Sophie put it, "Rat Boy thought every bar of music should be crammed with noise, and the audience should leave a gig with their nerve endings flayed. One of our reviews said: 'sounds like a group of crazed chimps slaughtering their pagan god.'"

Upbeat magazine asked me to do this sort of behind-the-scenes article about the band. Like, follow them around, ask some questions, all reality-TV style, except without a camera. Sophie and the Suprematists[1] —their new band name—were hot on the indie circuit, riding the ebbing tide of punk into something that didn't require mohawks, dog collars and shitloads of anger.

They had a new bass player, Pinky. Silent, like all bassists. He

---

[1]   Suprematism was a Russian art movement founded in 1913, focussed on basic geometric forms and "the supremacy of pure artistic feeling," rather than on visual depiction of objects, all of which nobody knew or gave a shit about.

played like an architect, layering up deep structure. He had a kind of stealth. Malice-free. He wasn't quite part of the group yet. Sophie had "found" him at the Blues House open-mic night. She thought he might be a closet jazzman, but he seemed to be able to slip into any genre. Everyone except Pinky knew her style: tragic, unstable, raw and wicked. Music scraped from the very organs of Sophonisba's[2] world. In just one song she could scream her guts out, cry a lyric or sing hysterically like a harpy. Every gig wiped her out. Every song exhausted her emotional arsenal.

"You know, everything was fine. Pinky was starting to fit in, but he thought the band should actually be, like, *practising*. He said we needed new songs. I agreed. He pissed off our drummer, Duke, when he said to him, 'What are you, a human sledgehammer?' I was reading about this leftist art movement in Russia. I wanted to write a song based on words by the poet Mayakovsky. There's this amazing recording of him reciting poetry like some doomsday oracle. 'I will sew myself black trousers from the velvet of my voice.' I loved that line. I don't know why, really. I didn't even quite get what it meant. But then I couldn't find the velvet in my voice let alone make black trousers from it!"

At that point she felt that structures of her world started to chunk off.

"It was, like, I know this sounds stupid but like my innards had dissolved. I couldn't access anything. There was no music, no words, no emotions, just this sloppy undefined mass. All I could do was cry or sit, catatonic, looking out the window all day. I couldn't write my angsty songs about love anymore and scream them into the mic. Rick was on my case constantly, and when we had sex he thrashed

---

2   Sophie's father, a classics professor, named her after Sophonisba, a Carthaginian noble-woman who lived during the Second Punic War and poisoned herself to avoid humiliation in a Roman triumph. This set the stage for Sophie's tragic disposition.

on me like I was the vessel of his sick inspiration. Some people, you know, never change. They just morph into more hideous versions of themselves."

She spent afternoons at Crank Coffee reading up on the Russians, especially Kulbin's idea of sensibility. She read me her favourite passage: "... the point where a subliminal sensation becomes conscious."

Meanwhile, crashing, head-banging straight-up power chord beats were giving way to a new rhythm and lyrics that seemed, she said, to alter the shape of her mouth. Pinky was cranking out new songs like a human jukebox. I went to their rehearsals, wielding my mini recorder. When Pinky listened to her struggle with a new song, he said, "It's in five, Soph; you can't cram it into a four-four. It's three-two, two-three, variable, like a man with a wooden leg walking down stairs."

She couldn't connect with her new music, so she started getting stage fright, throwing up before gigs, mangling words, disassociating in the middle of a song. Her tunes were impossible to slam dance to. Deprived of their body-smashing anger outlet, the audiences got bored. There were fewer and fewer bookings. The Suprematists—except Pinky, who stood in his corner plucking his celestial bass—were supremely frustrated. Sophie decided to take beta blockers, but they made her songs sound robotic, a pale whine in a loveless world. She tried downing four vodka-wheatgrass martinis before going onstage, but alcohol made her forget the lyrics, and she fumbled in glossolalia labyrinths of her own making. The band was constantly struggling to cover up, weed-whacking their way through chord changes. But Pinky could always lay down a bass solo that would float out like a magic carpet, bringing her back.

One night they were playing at the Stray Dog[3] on Broadland, a grubby hidey-hole venue with low ceilings and a fifties grotto vibe. They had this new schtick where Sophie would come onstage alone to sing the first few bars of their opening song, "Shitloads of Love." Sophie was freaking out about going onstage. On this occasion Pinky spoke, which was rare. He had a voice like a sedative, only a good one. "You wanna work on the intuitive principle, hon. Balance harmony with dissonance. Know how to use it, not let it use you." He smoothed his hands down the curves of his bass, then plucked out a little riff as an end-stop. Sophie gave him a zombie gaze, and I could tell she didn't really get what he was talking about. Pinky just stood there pulling on his goatee.

"Look, if you were a cow, it would be as simple as mooing. But you're a singer, so just sing."[4] Rat Boy stepped behind Sophie and tried to force something into her hand. Probably hash, his drug of choice. Look into this guy's eyes and all you see is Escher staircases that lead everywhere and nowhere. She didn't take it.

"When I walked onstage in my black velvet cape I felt like I'd passed through an invisible screen. Everything felt infused with reality. I looked out into the crowd in the dim light and it seemed like this mass of twitching and scuttling, pointing fingers, moving mouths, turning heads, like a weird chaos of interconnected sensory nodes, like a hive! I felt like I was going to sing to a room of insects and they were eating my songs; they were eating *me*."

---

3   FYI, Nikolai Kulbin founded the artists' cabaret *Stray Dog* in St. Petersburg, a key outlet for the Russian avant-garde from 1911–14. Sophie thought the owner of the Broadland bar was commemorating this hallowed venue. Actually, he renamed his bar Stray Dog after his wife threw him out of the house.

4   "...reveal our new souls in words as simple as mooing," lines from the prologue of Mayakovsky's futurist tragedy in verse, *Vladimir Mayakovsky*, in which urban despair is replaced, naturally, by utopian bliss, and the author was pelted by rotten eggs.

She came backstage and threw up. Rat Boy camouflaged himself in a corner. She watched the audience through a tiny slit in the curtain. Pinky came to her: "Hon, think threshold. Hold off on the ecstasy. This room is your habitat. These strangers come to hear you—the Emoto Queen—because that's their program, their deep need. All they need is a nudge, not a push. Music is like a pheromone. Your voice is a pheromone. They receive it like nectar from heaven." Then, because he wasn't holding his bass, he tapped out a little riff on her bare shoulder. She went back on and nailed it.

A few weeks later, Rat Boy dropped Sophie and dropped out. Pinky subbed in a female guitarist with a mean finger-picking style. The drummer started to lay off every few bars, carved out some space for himself. The Suprematists leapt back into indie play, but their style had changed: more plush, less catastrophic. They recorded their first CD. Pinky suggested the title: "Birth of the Velvet Voice," and everyone liked it except Sophie, who hadn't announced yet that she was carrying Pinky's child.

Man in the Moon

June 18. A man with a limp moved into the shack in old Mrs. Scott's backyard. Mom and Dad said to leave him alone. Now it's the Forbidden Zone.

June 19. We climbed over the fence. We waded commando-style through the grass. Rita waved her arms above her head, chanting, "Crimson and clover, over and over!" Lori and I did it too, spinning round and round in circles, "O-ver and o-ver..." till we crashed backwards to the ground, laughing. It felt like we were on a spinning planet. Lori—she's a risk-taker, Mom says—wanted to play the game where you pant and someone holds you from behind till you pass out. I did it once and it felt like going to heaven for, like, three seconds. Rita said it was stupid, you can wreck your brain doing it. Of course, Rita would never do anything that meant giving up control for one second of her life. Then she screeched, "Dirty old man, eats from a tin, likes to live in a garbage bin!" and the shack door opened. We all sucked in a breath and played dead in the grass. The shack man stepped out, lifting his one foot like a dead weight.

He bent down and chucked another empty tin can onto his pile. He looked over the yard with a cigarette hanging from his mouth. One shoulder slumped lower than the other one, and his hand was missing three fingers. He swung around and went back inside. Rita called him "Retard." I thought he looked harmless.

⌐

June 20. Our mission is ongoing. For the last few days we've been bugging the man in the shack. While we were supposedly making tie-dye T-shirts at Lori's, we snuck into the yard, threw rocks at the shack window and left dog poo on the porch. He ignored us and hulked about his solitary business. I thought it was getting too mean, but Rita and Lori, a.k.a. Dictator and Little Dictator, cooked up a new plan: we knock on his door and freak him out wearing ski masks.

Now it'll never happen. Today I fell off a chair. Dad was pointing, "Waxing crescent!" (he's teaching me phases of the moon) as I was try- ing to spot where the Apollo 11 astronauts would be landing. Which at that point was impossible cuz the moon looked like a white ba- nana. When I got up on tiptoes, I slipped off the edge of the chair and smashed to the floor like a chunk of space rock. I definitely felt like I was in a distant galaxy. My head hurts bad.

⌐

June 24. Mom and Dad said I had to stay inside and rest. Because of the concussion. I have a gash on the back of my head, like a zombie mouth. Which is kinda cool. I sat in bed all day reading a book about a boy who builds a cabin in the wilderness and survives on his own. I like boys' books because boys don't talk all the time. They go outside and actually do stuff and don't boss everybody around like the Two Dictators. It got me thinking how much I didn't miss my girlfriends.

Rita's so pushy and Lori's always out of control. They came to visit me, but all they could talk about was more ways to bug the hermit. I said they should leave him alone, but Rita pushed out her budding boobs and said, "Why don't you just marry him and live in outer space?" and dragged Lori off to find someone else they could torment.

July 8. I've been hanging out with Glenn from across the street. His dad is police chief. Glenn just loves marching around in his backyard with a fake rifle over his shoulder. Mister Law and Order. We play army games in his perfect backyard. He's teaching me how to make exploding grenade sounds. He says the shack man is a "commo," whatever that means. Glenn and his wispy brother are seriously allergic to everything. Their house is like a hospital ward—shiny waxed floors, covers on the furniture, everything preserved like a crime scene. Their mother wipes out every tiny life form from every surface. But I still like Glenn. He doesn't talk too much. Not like Rita. I can hear her voice half a block away, puncturing the air. Dad calls her the Human Megaphone.

July 12. Gave up on Glenn. Same games every day. No imagination. Being a soldier seems like the most boring thing ever. I'm watching the shack now. Today the hermit finally came out. In his non-gimpy hand, he held up a mousetrap and mouthed the word "mice." He held the mouse above the fence so I could see its little crushed skull. We shared our first word!

July 15. I thought maybe at some point the hermit might talk to me. I stole some stuff from home to leave him as presents. He never saw me put them on his doorstep, but he knew it was me. Small stuff: a packet of Tang, an old fountain pen (maybe he's a writer!), a cocktail thingie shaped like a samurai sword that said "Hy's Steakhouse" on it. When he sees me over the fence, he nods, no expression on his face. I nod, too. Our secret pact.

July 16. Apollo liftoff. Holy cow.

July 17. Tonight Mom and Dad stayed up to watch Apollo 11. I couldn't sleep, so they let me sit with them on the couch and eat Ritz crackers. Collins said to NASA that after a while you get tired of banging off the ceilings and walls. The earth looked like a tiny SuperBall from space. Dad said, "Just think! One day we might all live on the moon!" Always the dreamer.

July 18. The shack man came out. He was wearing an army jacket (on one arm, anyway), and his hair was all neat. He left in a taxi. I don't know why I did it, but I snooped in the shack. He never locked it. There were cigarette papers everywhere, like little strips of paper from fortune cookies, only blank. I saw the pen I gave him. Or parts of it. In the corner there was a worn-out armchair and an ashtray full of cigarette butts stubbed into ash dunes. In front of the chair on a table there was a big black radio with the cover off, wires sprouting from the insides. There was a headphone thing beside it, stuff pulled out like two dislocated eyeballs. Maybe this is what he works on at night when his light's on, taking things apart like my dad, except that shack man never puts them back together again. While I was poking around, an ambulance wailed down the street and all the dogs started howling. Some half-dead person was probably hanging from a rescue rope somewhere. Then the shack man just stomped right in. I never heard a car. He pointed to the radio and said it was his. "Fixed it."

I was trapped behind the chair. The siren faded away. He said they called him through the wires. "They're going to the moon. Lunar module-five." I just kept nodding. Then he told me I should go, and held the door open. He looked like a badly stuffed scarecrow in his uniform, but I could tell he liked wearing it.

For a first meeting it was a bit weird. I thought he might be mad at me, but I don't think he was. I was amazed he could fix the radio. It gave me an idea.

July 19. The astronauts flew past the Smythe Sea and over moon craters that looked like bubbles in a pot of white sauce.

I stole a box from Dad's clock workshop. An old alarm clock, taken apart, but all the pieces were there. I climbed the fence with the box wrapped in my shirt. But when I went to put it on the shack man's doorstep, I hit a can on the top of his pile and it rolled down to the cement, ka-clunk, ka-clunk. The door opened. The shack man stood there staring at me. Our faces were close. His was scarred with pock-marks. One pupil was bigger. When he leaned forward, he reached out his two-fingered hand to me. I was crouching, one hand holding the can, the other one holding the box. He looked down at the stuff in the box, then at me. His mouth was weird, like an invisible thread underneath his skin pulled the muscles in all the wrong directions.

He kind of lost his balance and jerked forward. I thought he was mad. I thought he was lunging for me. I scrambled backwards, dropped the box, got to my feet and ran, ripping the skin off my knee climbing over the fence.

When I got to the house, Mom yelled, "What happened?" But the shack man's weird face was still haunting me. She followed me into the bedroom and asked if I fell off the fence. I nodded. She asked if I was bothering the man or if he was bothering me. I answered yes but didn't say to which question.

When Dad got home from work, he came straight to my bedroom. "Hello there, earthling!" I told him I had a sliver in my knee. He got out his pointiest watchmaker tweezers, found the end of the sliver and pulled it out.

"Cedar. They're the worst." My dad fixes everything. The three of us had our wiener roast in the fireplace like we did every Friday. We sat there like demons, waiting for the red skin to blister and brown. Dad said he would set up my pool on the weekend. Mom said to me, "Just leave the shack man alone now."

⁓

July 20. Moonwalk! Dad opened a bottle of bubbly (I got a tiny bit) and we all toasted Aldrin and Armstrong as they bounced around on the moon. I saw the Two Dictators at Evelyn Park today, hogging the big swings, but I avoided them.

⁓

July 21. Haven't talked to the shack man. But I still keep an eye on him and try to hear if he's had more radio contact from the moon. There's a heat wave. Eighty-five degrees! Across the street, all the neighbour-hood kids in their wet bathing suits are playing Red Rover. "Red Rover,

Red Rover, I call whoever over!" I hate that game. It's nasty. Us against them. The little kids always end up crying. There was a snakeskin in front of our house, like the snake had just crossed the road and left his old clothes behind.

July 22. Labelled my rock collection and then went outside to paddle in my pool. Green with orange tropical fish! Dad says the moon has a crater called the Sea of Tranquility. I like sticking my head under the water. It makes the world up there feel so far away. Just me. When you walk under water it looks the same as an astronaut walking in space, like the way you would walk in a dream. I decided I'm like the hermit, only more normal. People aren't who you think they are. Like even I could be a boy, not a girl.

July 24. The astronauts brought back a bunch of moon rocks. Do they hover in the air if you throw them? Dad's *National Geographic* says the earth has its own note. Like if you went thirty octaves below the middle C on a piano, that's the note. But humans can't hear it. But maybe we can feel it. Like a freighter that's really far away and the vibrations go through the ocean and suddenly your mood changes.

July 28. A fire engine screamed by to the canyon again. Probably useless boys trapped in the undertows or stupid tourists stepping off the cliffs to doom. Half the neighbourhood—and of course Rita and her smudgy brothers—ran down there to rubberneck. Rita has a thing for smashed-in heads. Her parents are professional looky-loos, when they're not busy drinking at the Legion. A girl from my school who lives a block away disappeared. No one has a clue where she is. Probably buried in the woods somewhere.

〜

August 6. The police came to the shack. They knocked but he didn't answer. He would have answered if it was me. Dad went to the police auction and bought me a blue, three-speed Raleigh bike. Which is cool.

〜

August 8. It's hot. I'm sleeping with just a sheet on. I looked out my window to check if the shack man's light was on, but it was dark. It's been dark for the last three nights. I wonder why. I wonder if he ever got the clock back together again, if he knows what a mainspring is, or a stem-winder. What frequency is the moon?

Mom and Dad are watching TV. I can hear them talking. Mom says something like *living in that shack. He's finally gone.* She asks Dad a question. Something about Korea and "shell-shocked." He says, *couldn't even smile, poor man.*

I'm staring at the ceiling, following every upside-down hill and valley. I have this ache that hurts my chest. Like someone's pressing down on it and I can't stop them. The night light is shining up the wall. The white plaster up there looks like the surface of a lonely planet.

"Magnificent desolation." That's what Aldrin said about the moon.

Magicicada

Jean's eighty-three. She never sleeps through the night anymore. She gets up at 5:00 a.m. to swim in Magic Lake.

There are those who swim for pleasure. And those who swim for exercise. Jean is neither. She swims for survival. As a form of prayer. She goes into the water as an unexpectant initiate. The moment she slips into the lake's green depths in her now thirty-year-old one-piece, she allows her body to be embraced by the water. Sometimes she dips underwater and swims with just her legs, the surface quivering like quicksilver atop. She swims as long or as little as it takes to make her skin feel new. When she's done, she dries off under the ash trees and walks the fifteen minutes back to her house.

In a wicker chair on her small back deck, she waits for the sun to come up. She used to take a sherry after her swim. No need to toast the dawn anymore. She wants only to hear the song of the emerging seventeen-year cicadas. It may be the last time. A molten band of morning light blooms up from the eastern horizon.

In 1944, the same year Virginia's seventeen-year Brood I cicadas came out in full force, Jean was thirty-two and married. She had a child, a boy. Her second one, actually. At age twenty-two she'd given birth out of wedlock and given the infant girl away to adoption. That's what was done back then. The girl wrote to her a few years ago, but Jean had never answered. Her husband, Ted, named their son George. Then, as the boy's medical problems became apparent, promptly left her. He sent money, but not love. The neighbourhood kids called her son Gimpy George. She knew. Those were different times. People grimaced or looked the other way when she pushed him in the pram around town, his loud bellowing belying his small size. In those days you kept a disabled child out of public view. But she didn't care.

George never learned to walk or talk, but he loved the water. He had good strong arms for a child. In the summer when everyone in the neighbourhood was inside eating dinner, Jean would take George to Magic Lake. She couldn't remember if this really was the name of the lake or if she had named it that for Georgie's sake. First they would sit on the dock under the ash tree and listen to the blackbirds. She told him about the day he was born and how everywhere in the woods the Blue Ridge cicada nymphs were crawling up trees in the hundreds to shed their skins and become adults; how this very ash tree had vibrated with the songs of the *Magicicada*. She wasn't sure he understood. Then she would carry him to the lake and wade into the shallows. Skimming him across the surface on his back, she pretended he was a boat, or a dolphin, or a shark, and he flopped his arms in delight. Never did she let him feel that he would sink if she let go.

When George turned ten, he was getting too heavy for her to carry and move around. He could sit for hours in his chair and stare out the window at some far-off place. She started to put a piece of paper and pen on the tray in front of him, and he filled the pages with frantic lines and circles. Childish scribbles, but she kept most of them. Later, when she missed him, she would pull one out of the drawer and look at it, feeling the frenetic energy inside his body, studying the pen marks to access the mystery of his thoughts. As he got older, Georgie started to rage at her and strike her in the face. It was as if he knew they would soon have to be separated. Or perhaps it was his way of speaking something urgent. They still got letters from Ted then, and the occasional package with some inappropriate gift for George she always had to give away: a baseball glove, roller skates, team jerseys. It was as if Ted was trying to negate George by sending him normal boy things. When Ted wrote that his "other" son was learning to ride a bike, she cried. But she read the letter out loud to George—even the parts about the boy careering wobbly down the driveway—and he made his funny cronking laugh, as if he saw the whole thing a different way.

There was a day, years ago, when she gave her son a small mirror to hold in his hand. He was still and stared into it for a long time with an expression of astonishment. She was never sure whether he recognized himself, or whether he felt communion with the reflection of a stranger.

When George was admitted to the Roanoke County Care Home, he was surprisingly quiet. She was pleased to see that his room would look out on a large pond where ducks and geese floated lazily amidst the lily pads. And there were blackbirds. He would like that. Afterwards, when she missed him terribly, she would go to the lake for a swim. This is when the ritual started. A long, slow exhale standing on shore, then—immersion in the landscape, all sound receding. Time in her body, her strokes marking passage, a small splash of each hand as it cut through the lake's surface. She'd float on her back and listen to the wind in the ash tree. And, in season, the frogs. She heard in their croaks and calls the joy in George's voice. A language understood by intimates. People said she should have had another child, a "normal" one. They didn't know about the previous child. But she felt the world she had shared with George was not something to replace.

⌒

George died one Sunday afternoon in July, age seventeen. It was hot that summer. The ground was still littered with cicada casings. The woman who phoned from the home seemed evasive. Jean had to jam the receiver against her ear to understand:

"Mrs. Barker?" the woman had said. "George... there was an incident this afternoon... we don't know how."

"How what?" Jean had asked, not wanting to hear the answer.

There was a long breath from the other end. "He wheeled out to the pond somehow... he must have dragged himself in."

"You mean he drowned? Georgie drowned?"

"Yes, Mrs. Barker. I'm sorry. Maybe he wanted to... well, it was an accident."

She'd hung up the phone. *If only she'd been there to hold him up in the water as she used to.* Days passed when all she could do was sit in her armchair, remembering those humid days with her son when time hung like thick strands from the trees.

Ted came to the funeral, much to her surprise. "Poor little fella," he had said. "Now his suffering's over." Jean had flown at him in a rage. "He was not little! He was seventeen!" She lashed out at him, spitting out the frustration from years of isolation. The funeral party had instantly dispersed. They had never been a part of Georgie's world. She stood alone, then, at the grave site. The whirring cicadas filled the trees in the cemetery, their strange humming like the engine of a mother ship.

The sun has risen. More than risen. She fell asleep waiting. And with the warmth from the light, a single cicada is the first to whirr into song. Gradually more cicadas join, until the sound becomes a high-pitched call orchestrating the morning. It seems to enter her through the soles of her feet, channel up her spine and exit out the top of her head. She is electric field, charged matter, mourning mother all at once. The song energizes at first. And then at a crucial threshold, it enervates. She goes inside.

Her left hip hurts. Her world feels paper-thin, at risk of being torn by the slightest wind. Her feet take her to the dresser in the living room where she retrieves one of Georgie's last drawings. Still in her bathing suit, she sits down on the couch facing the window, the view he would have had. Outside, the yellow jackets swarm, flying aggressively back and forth between the fruit trees, tracing jagged paths in the air. It looks like the angry scribbles Georgie had made on the paper. In fact, the more she looks, the more she becomes convinced that he was drawing the wasps' flight path. There are distinct forward-moving vector lines and intermittent zig-zags, a furious searching and seeking pattern. She looks at the backside of the paper: August 1954. The mad heat of summer. The heavy air. She turns the paper over again, staring at the drawing, feeling what worlds her son had occupied inside his muteness.

She gets up and returns the drawing to the cabinet drawer. At the back is the letter she received two years ago, from her daughter, right around George's birthday. She had not replied. Then, it had seemed an issue too far in the past to address. But today it feels different.

She pours herself a sherry, sits down at the table and opens the letter. There's a smaller envelope inside that she had missed the first time. It contains a photo: her adult daughter in a one-piece bathing suit and swim cap, standing by a lake. The caption on the back side reads: *Lake Michigan, 60 km Swim Challenge.* Jean flips the photo over several times. Even the handwriting looks like hers. She starts writing a response. "Dear Angela. I am sorry it's taken me so long to write. The facts about your birth are, of course, correct. If you would like to meet me, I live in Virginia, in Roanoke County. Also, I would like you to know that you had a half-brother, George. He lived with me in this house. I don't know what else to say other than I am very pleased to hear from you after all these years...."

End of the Line

Today Kurt saw the girl from the 222. Still blonde and slim. She was walking uphill toward him with an elderly man. Her father? Despite being in her fifties by now, he recognized her instantly, his body flooding with a flash of long-forgotten lust and a pang of fear. He pretended to yank on the dog's leash as a distraction, but as the woman passed she looked directly at him, coldly, as if her blue eyes were made of glass.

In the past, he thought that look was youthful disdain. He remembered the first time he saw her, at Kelman Park with her girlfriends, her long, tanned legs dangling from the zip-line as she zoomed on a cable to the other side. She was different from the others. There was something contained about her, as if she carried within her a deep hidden realm he wanted to discover. Everybody leaves a trace, a chemical marker wherever they go. Trails that repel or attract others. She certainly had a trail.

Trails are what led him back here to Vancouver's North Shore. So many walking trails that led into the woods and up the mountain. Trails through secret parks and along power lines, hidden groves of old cedars. That, and some residue of nostalgia that lingered. The way the low clouds hung on the slopes in winter. The mountain's presence, solid and mystical. It was a place you could merge with, hunker down in. He didn't even want to cross the bridge into downtown anymore. He was content to observe the pulse of the city from afar.

Kurt walked his dog every day in the shadow of those mountains, their glowering blue, often under a sky weeping rain, which was typical of the West Coast. Drooping red cedars, flicker-pecked snags, and coyotes that roamed the golf courses, snapping the heads off cats. A melancholy that felt pleasantly anesthetizing. At seventy-six he was in good shape, but Trixie was getting old. Sometimes he had to yank on the leash to propel her, or even slap her on the backside. He still walked past the old bus stop from his former route, the 222, *the end of the line*. The route no one wanted because there was nothing to do but sit on the bus for twenty minutes before the next shift. Or go to the park for a smoke, which is what he did. That's how he got to know who roamed the neighbourhood. Thirty years ago the houses were smaller and more spaced apart. Now they all looked identical—ugly "builders' specials" that took up entire lots. Back then there weren't as many parked cars, and the kids wandered everywhere by themselves, even barefoot in summer in their cut-off shorts, hiding in the parks, smoking pot, fondling each other. There was graffiti everywhere, late-night parties in the bush, secret gangs. Teenagers made the air crackle, especially the girls.

A few days ago a group of local boys had found a skull up by Rice Lake, only a hundred feet from the trail. Covered in several decades' worth of fir needles. Their dog had spotted a corner of the comforter it had been wrapped in, sticking up from the soil. The newspaper said the boys had been playing with the skull on their street when a parent had intervened. Kurt doesn't walk in that area.

He headed down to the community centre. One of the local dog walkers had recommended an older-dog obedience class after seeing him drag Trixie by the collar to get her to move. He had signed up. Today was the first day.

"Just by being with your dog you teach him how to behave. What we want, people, is good socialization," said the instructor, a woman in her forties with a toned body. They went around the room and each dog owner said what behaviours they would like to change.

"Biting."

"Attacking other dogs for no reason."

"Just really weird irrational behaviour."

When it came to Kurt, he drew a blank.

"Take your time," the instructor said.

He looked down at Trixie. "Too timid."

⁓

One day all those years ago, the blue-eyed girl with the long legs had got on his bus and gone all the way to Ambleside Beach. She hadn't noticed him. But he certainly had noticed her. And he'd made sure when he finished his shift a half-hour later to drive down there in his car and "happen upon her." Young girls don't usually detect those kinds of coincidences. He'd offered to drive her home. Of course he knew generally where she lived.

The girl's waist—he still couldn't remember her name—had been impossibly small, her torso long. He would say she was almost gangly, not quite grown into her body. She had worn ridiculous jeans with buttons instead of a zipper, some latest teen fashion that would vex his dexterity.

He said he just needed to stop at his place for something. She wanted to wait in the car but, assuring her he wasn't an ogre, he invited her in, introduced her to his housemate who was slouched on the sofa, flicking his lighter on and off, on and off. As they chatted casually, he gave her a tour of the house (which was nothing special), led her to the basement room with the mattress that was supposed to be temporary, the naked walls, the wood bug carcasses heaped in the webby corners.

He always slept well there, in his end-of-the-line rooming house.

When he touched her she seemed to suddenly go into a trance. He took this as a good sign. Unlike the others, she didn't fight him. She surrendered, as something small and fragile might succumb to ethylene vapours in a jar. He undressed her, smacked her on the bottom, then holding her by the shoulders got her down on the floor and stripped off his clothes. He stood over her. Her face was turned away, toward the small window on the far wall. Outside, a lawn mower droned. His erection poised, he'd hesitated, asked her age. Jesus Christ. He apologized and drove her home, dropping her off a block away. *Don't tell your parents.*

The dog owners were trailing out of the community centre when the instructor called him back.

"Kurt, could I have a word with you? Bring Trixie."

He walked across the gym floor to the instructor, yanking on the dog's leash.

"Your discipline is not consistent. Sometimes it's too harsh. How old is Trixie?"

"About thirteen or fourteen."

"Well, I think she may be in pain. And her collar's too tight."

He looked down at his dog and her rheumy eyes, surprised that she might be feeling something.

"Have you taken her to the vet recently for a checkup?"

He hadn't. Not recently. Not for four or five years. She did whatever she was told to do mostly, except on walks.

He walked Trixie home, back up the steep hill, which was really the flank of the mountain. The hill seemed longer and steeper than it ever had before. When he jerked the leash to get Trixie to move faster, she yelped. The collar. He bent down and adjusted the buckle so that it hung more loosely. There was a years-old band of matted fur around her neck and patches of raw skin. She looked up at him with her sad, rheumy eyes. At the street's upper terminus hikers vanished into the woods. *Buttons instead of a zipper.* Beverly. That was the girl's name.

The sky was stark blue. He felt self-consciously visible. From above, the mountain loomed with a brute presence. One of the retired dog walkers waved from the other side of the road, then crossed over to talk to him.

"You're sure giving the old girl a workout...."

Kurt kept walking. The closer he got to his street, the weaker and more reluctant the dog became. Had he pushed her too hard these last few years? He bent down and picked her up. She was much lighter than he expected her to be, almost skeletal under all that fur. When he rounded the corner to his house there was a police car parked between his home and the neighbour's. The officer unbuckled his seat belt as Kurt turned into the driveway. Along the path to the front door, Trixie trembled in his arms.

The Sheen of Ice on Snow

Her husband took the car. There was a trail of red dots in the snow from his bleeding hand. She had never been so quick with a knife. She had never been anything with a knife. It snowed all evening after he left, all night and again in the morning. The lights in the cottage flashed on and off, as if a frisson of anger kept frying the wires.

She lit the wood stove, part of Harlon's original fantasy about country living—having your own woodlot, hunting your own meat—an experiment that had failed within the first year and forced them to move back to the city. The cabin was mostly a summer place now, not really fit for the colder months, except for short stays. Since last fall they'd been stuck in an alternating dynamic of explosive anger or despair. They had thought coming back would help them deal with their daughter's disappearance six months ago. Instead, they'd had a monumental argument yesterday when Harlon had proposed they get rid of the cottage.

She stuffed his "Ah! The Element of Surprise" chemistry T-shirt he'd left behind into the stove. The flames ate holes through the fabric. It must be fifteen years old by now. He'd taken up wearing it again, she wasn't sure why. A nostalgia thing? Trying to look youthful—to someone?

Yesterday, when he'd come back inside he wouldn't speak to her. He'd gone straight for the bedroom, probably to pack, and she had blocked his way, still holding the paring knife. She'd screamed at him that they weren't selling. All he'd said was, *For Christ's sake. Stop it. She's gone.* When he grabbed her to move her aside she'd pushed him. The knife blade had caught his right hand.

Standing by the kitchen window, Julia let the falling flakes pass before her eyes. The knife was still there on the kitchen counter, with the dried blood on its tip. She should have washed it but she didn't. Instead, she shoved it to the back of the utensil drawer. It was still snowing heavily. The road was disappearing. You couldn't see much beyond it, no houses or power poles. The familiar numbness started to fill her body. She welcomed it back.

Something at the back of the property caught her eye. A red fox sitting upright on a mound with his front legs straight, his tail swiped to the side, eyes closed as if in meditation. His fur glowed against the snow. He seemed to be listening, homing in, his ears swivelling to focus on a sound she couldn't hear from inside. Maybe somewhere under the snow cover small prey were stirring. He got on all fours. Then, in one liquid movement, he pounced.

⌐

Harlon didn't call. At twilight a figure came roaming up the hill, wading through the deep snow. An old woman in a coat. Her legs were bare.

"Hello, hello! I wonder, may I use your toilet?"

Julia invited her inside.

"Snow like borax crystals in the air..." the old woman said, as she brushed off her coat.

"You talk like a chemist!" Julia laughed, helping her off with her jacket.

"*Lilly's Nana Kills Rubbish Creatures Frantically,*" the woman answered, with her index finger raised. "Alkali metals."

Julia hung the wet coat over a chair. "Were you out in this blizzard?"

"Well, I was out on my walk and took... a turn," the old woman said. "I live over there," she gestured vaguely to the north.

"No gloves?"

"Oh no, this is not cold to me at all," the old woman answered, her lips beginning to turn blue.

"My husband is a chemist," Julia said. The old woman did not look around to see if the husband was there. Julia chose to not reveal his hasty departure. "Although we don't always get along. Yesterday he said to me, *As friends, we worked well as an emulsion. But as husband and wife, we're immiscible.*" She had laughed at his words but hated that she couldn't quite remember what "immiscible" meant. She knew it wasn't good.

When Julia asked if the old woman knew, she answered, "It means..." and drew a finger across her throat. Julia pointed her to the washroom.

The old woman accepted Julia's offer of warmer clothes: Harlon's Shetland sweater and his fleece pants. The woman sat there like a Harlon effigy by the wood stove, eating pistachios from the dish Julia had given her.

As Julia stoked the fire, the old woman got up and went to the bookshelf. She picked up a photo and waving it about said, "Isn't it nice to feel young."

"That's my daughter Kristina, eleven years old. She went—" Julia took it from the old woman and repositioned it exactly as it had been on the shelf.

The old woman had a vague way of speaking. It annoyed Julia at first. But then she realized the woman had lost her ability for specifics. She used words as signifiers for other words because she couldn't remember the names of things. This made her sound oddly poetic. "I like it there, over in the white land," she had said, gesturing out the window, as if speaking in an old language altered by translation.

The old woman got the master bedroom that night, and Julia slept in Kristina's bed.

In the morning Julia heard the old woman get up before her, then fell back into a deep sleep, into a dream in which she disguised herself in an oversized coat with a fur hood that almost suffocated her.

At ten Julia got up and dressed. Snow fell in a muffling flurry. The old woman burst through the front door, stamping her feet. She was wearing Harlon's huge mukluks, and looked like some Mongolian herdswoman, calm and resilient, indifferent to the past or the future. As she entered, her cheeks red with the cold, she extended her bare hand to Julia and placed an object in Julia's palm, saying, "For you." It looked like something the cat had coughed up. But on closer inspection it turned out to be an owl pellet filled with undigested fur and twig-like bones, tiny femurs and mandibles, the remnants of small forest dwellers. In a low voice, Julia thanked the old woman. With the pellet nestled in her palm, she then walked with her hand extended out from her body, not looking at the pellet, and went to the living room where she placed it on the bottommost shelf of the bookcase where it wouldn't be seen.

They played cards to pass the time, ate canned peaches, and cracked open the whisky even though Julia was not much of a drinker. They started with Gin Rummy, a family favourite, but the woman seemed baffled by the rules. Julia switched it to Go Fish. The stove crackled, and snow accumulated on the fence posts and trees, on the roof and on the roads.

"Julia, do you have an ace?"

"Go Fish."

"Do you have a five?"

"Go Fish."

It was not an adult game. And it was impossible to play strategically with only two people. She had her suspicions that the old woman was not surrendering cards from her hand when she had them. They reached an impasse, gave up, and sat enjoying the fire, drifting off in the muted day.

In the late afternoon a snowmobile came labouring up the drive. A man got off and before he could come up to the door Julia bounded out to meet him. Inside, the old woman was flipping through old issues of Kristina's *Chickadee* magazines.

"Hi. I'm Phil Langston. I'm just wondering if you've seen my mother around. She lives a couple of miles over that way," he pointed, southward. "We just popped by to visit her and she wasn't there. Small lady, with a navy blue coat." He scowled. "Shouldn't be out on her own."

Julia smelled alcohol on his breath. He kept flicking his shiny black hair as the wind lifted it across his face. The snowflakes stuck to his black lashes. There was a sort of lustre to him, like the sheen of ice on snow.

Standing with her body blocking the stairs, she lied to him about the old woman, saying she had seen her on their summer visits. But not lately. She also lied about her husband, saying he was due to return this afternoon and they would both keep an eye out. The words flowed out effortlessly. He handed her his card then offered to help shovel the drive, but she assured him she was going to do it before dark. Just as he turned to leave she called, "I hope you find her." Her words hung there in the frigid air.

Would he entrap the old woman? Lock her up, no more walkabouts and whisky? Julia didn't feel ready to surrender her new house guest. Truth be told, she hadn't really engaged with any of the locals before. There used to be a ceramics artist down by the lake and, to the west, a gay couple who threw huge summer parties. She didn't know if any of them still lived here now that the hordes of retired urbanites had arrived.

After the man left, she went behind the cabin and chopped wood ferociously as if cracking the skulls of enemy marauders.

"I'm not interested in that," said the woman when Julia came in bearing firewood. "They want me to move. I won't do it."

"Don't worry. I shooed him away. You're safe for now." Julia had the impression the old woman was sequestering the truth from herself, but she let it slide.

—

For dinner Julia heated up noodles and wieners. "My husband loves wieners," she said as she put the plates down on the table, "Even if he knows what's in them." They both plunged into their meal. The old woman ate mechanically without stopping. The way a child would eat too much of one thing and get sick. Since she'd arrived at the cottage, Julia herself had started eating this way.

Julie put down her fork. "I met Harlon in a chemistry class at Carleton. I ruined his first lab project. When we started dating I noticed his arms were shorter than mine and when we walked holding hands my left shoulder always stuck up, like this. It always felt so *awkward*, like I was stuck inside a coat hanger."

The old woman laughed and winked. "My husband liked the missionary position."

Later they dipped into the whisky again and polished off two tins of smoked oysters and a box of fancy crackers. "Why do these round things have holes?" the old woman asked, lifting one up for inspection.

"So when you hold them to the light you see tiny stars." Soon the old woman drifted off sitting in the armchair. Julia's numbness returned.

At first Julia was angry that Harlon had left her the way he had—

carless, during a snowstorm. But then she came to see that the drama and finality of it made it easier. She had no way of countering his gesture, which would merely have perpetuated their feud. Deep inside she still liked the *idea* of Harlon, a stand-alone Harlon, a Harlon without the wonky framework of their relationship. He was earnest but so insistent that for them to survive they needed to "kill off their old selves" and start all over. *Maybe. But not until they found Kristina.*

Framed in the black window, the snow streamed down like a film whose once-clear images had faded to blurry streaks. She refused to think of snow as a covering over of the past, a new beginning. No, it was just another overlay of the shifting landscape that was her life.

At nine p.m. the power went out temporarily. With only a few candles to light the room it was impossible to read.

"I'll give you a start," said the old woman.

"Okay."

"There once was a... field."

"Uh, a field. Okay. There was a field. A large field." Julia felt a bit stumped where to go next. "It's full of little round holes. A woman is looking in these holes for something. Small animals. Or birds."

"What's her name?" the old woman asked.

"Uh. Violet."

"That's *my* name," the old woman said. But Julia didn't believe her.

"She, uh, Violet, looks down one of these holes and sees a young fox with a bushy feather-duster tail. She pulls him out, holds him in her arms and strokes his tail, which the fox seems to like, since he doesn't wake from his winter sleep. The plain has a golden light that lights the fields and trees. Violet walks, holding the fox in her arms. There's a red silo...."

"Oh! Are we in the prairies?"

"Uh, sure, yes, the prairies. Standing by the red silo there's a farmer with a beat-up truck. 'Oh, so ya found ma fox,' he says. 'Is it yours?' she asks. 'Yes,' he says, so she hands it to him. 'I been lookin' for one like that fer years!'" Julia was quite enjoying being a narrator. It had been a while since she had told a story. "Violet regrets giving up the fox. Maybe he wants to skin it for its fur, she thinks. The guy offers her a ride. 'To where?' she asks. She doesn't have a clue where she is. 'Jes to town.' The guy winks with his crocodile eye. Violet doesn't trust him. He drives with the fox in his lap, stroking it like a cat—"

The old woman had fallen asleep sitting up, her mouth open, like a child. Julia left her there undisturbed and went to sleep on Kristina's bed. Sometime in the night she heard the old woman wandering inside the cottage. Julia got up and led her to the main bedroom, gave her a spare nightie and put her to bed.

⟶

Today was the shortest day, Julia remembered. Or the longest night, depending on how you looked at it. Lately, every night seemed like the longest night. She assumed the old woman was still asleep and thought a sleep-in would do her good. Maybe today she should call the woman's son. She eased herself off the small bed and went to the kitchen. In the low morning light the snow had an inner blue glow, as if a tiny lamp were buried inside it. Why did prophets always appear out of a desert? Why not from an expanse of snow? Winter, it seemed to her, was a much better time to be wandering around alone, weaving the strands of some grand philosophy.

There were fresh footprints leading out the front door, veering off into the woods. The old woman had gone out in the cold. Harlon's snow boots were gone. The woman's coat was still on the hook. Julia put a jacket on and went outside to look for her. She kept slipping through the snow crust, fooled each time by the seeming solidity of the drifts, calling out the woman's name, which may or may not have been Violet. But the snow-laden trees seemed to dampen her calls. She felt a tiny stab of panic in her chest and stood for a moment in her deep footprints. She'd thought she would know in her body whether Kristina was still alive, but she didn't. A huge discharge of loose snow plummeted off a branch from above.

The tracks circled back to the woodshed behind the cottage where their acreage spread out like frozen sand dunes shaped by the wind, punctuated by the thin trunks of birch trees. Julia saw the old lady there, standing in a corner of the woodshed, her neck craned upward. Wearing only Harlon's boots and a nightie. She was examining a spider web. *No doubt, she was once a sharp woman, a chemist with a good job.* Julia held back and watched, marvelling at how the woman found pleasure in the tiniest, most mundane things. She approached and said, "Good morning," but the old woman stayed transfixed. It looked as if the spider was in the web, but it was a dried exoskeleton from months ago. The old woman turned and said, "Isn't it beautiful still."

Julia coaxed her back inside and got her dressed, but the woman was fidgety, unable to sit. Seeing this, Julia offered, "How about the two of us go for a stroll over the hill to the lake? We'll have to trudge a bit, but it's not that far." As they walked away from the cottage, she wondered if Harlon would come back. This thought made her feel less numb.

When they crested the hill, the icy expanse of the lake spread out before them. Everything from the lake to the hills to the trees rimmed around the shore was awash in a lurid light. They took the trail down to the shore.

"Look! Someone's camping!" Violet pointed to a shelter on the ice. She walk-skated wobbily toward the tent. "Hello!" she shouted, waving her arms for balance. "Hello, hello!"

A head popped out.

"May we look inside?" the old woman asked.

"Sure. C'mon in. I'm Bob. And this here is Allen." The two men sat on a wooden bench, one threading an inch-long shiner onto his hook, the other holding his baited line and looking down into the eerie green light at his feet.

"This is, uh, my mother, Violet," Julia said, surprised at her own lie. "And I'm Julia."

They all nodded. Bob pulled up another bench. Allen looked directly across at Julia. He had solid brown eyes, like discs of milk chocolate. He was surveying her like someone who had just whitewashed a wall and then stood back to see what spots had been missed. A heater sent out waves of warmth.

"Are you from around here?" Julia asked.

"Nope. Drove down from Hope's Landing."

"Don't you get bored sitting around waiting for the fish to bite?"

Allen looked down into the circle of light. "Ice fishing's all about biding your time. Good day for walleyes, though. Wind's up and the water's ruffled. That's how they like it—murky."

"They got mirror eyes. Can see prey in the dark," Bob added.

They all sat watching the watery hole.

"Are the fish still alive in the... frozen time?" the old woman inquired in her odd poetic way.

"Oh sure. They're cold-blooded, unlike us humans. Got their own nature's thermostat."

Allen's rod twitched ever so slightly. His eyes darted to the ice hole.

"Bob, we got game." The rod bent sharply downward.

"Ladies and gentlemen, we got ourselves a pickerel!"

"Walleye," Allen corrected.

"But how can you tell?" Julia wondered.

"Well," Bob butted in, "See how the rod bows, pulls down. Perch would rip it right off. Nope. We got a *pickerel*. Haul 'er up, Allen."

Allen reeled in the catch, a long, greenish fish with a ridgy lizard-like dorsal fin, almost prehistoric-looking, and gently removed it from the hook, as if he were unbuttoning a woman's blouse. "Walleye," he repeated.

Bob took it to a metal basin, whacked it on the head and quickly wrapped it in newspaper.

"For you, ladies."

Violet took the package. "Well, you just never know what you get when you go fish. Either way, someone's got to die."

Allen glanced at Julia, eyebrows raised.

On the way back, snow started to come fast and thick again. The clouds closed in. The shortest day was all too short.

Julia undid the wrapping around the walleye. Although dead, it still looked beautiful, its iridescent scales shimmering olive green and yellow. Its eyes were fixed in a neutral stare. A feeling of alarm welled up from her bowels, but she suppressed it. She opened the utensil drawer and pretended not to see the stained knife from two days ago lingering at the back, instead reaching for a filleting knife. Filleting was not her strong point. If Harlon were here he would fillet it like a pro while waving around a glass of wine in one hand and spooling out some long-winded story. She did a bad job of it, but she did it.

Julia fried the fish for dinner. When they were putting the dishes away, she told Violet that she and Harlon have a little sailboat that they take out on the lake in the summer. He liked to get out in "the elements." It was a thrill to glide, sails full, across the water to the other side. Where there was nothing, really, only a weedy area. Oddly, at the very moment Julia told this, she felt a great love for Harlon and his fervour to embrace the new. But in her telling, she had left out the family's most avid sailor, her daughter, Kristina, who had gone missing from the cottage in July.

Julia drank a lot that night while Violet slept slumped in the armchair, wearing Harlon's sweater. The snow was wet and heavy now, coming down in audible grey blobs. The fire died down.

Julia's phone vibrated. She leaned over sleepily to look. From Harlon. "Jules. They found her body."

Acknowledgements

Thank you to Vici Johnstone of Caitlin Press for believing in this manuscript and, along with Caitlin staff Sarah Corsie and Monica Miller, for breathing it into life and sending it out to the greater world.

I owe a huge debt of gratitude to Cathleen With, my Vancouver Manuscript Intensive mentor, for always believing in my writing. Peter Gelfin of The Editorial Department cast his sharp eye for craft on my writing and brought me up to a new level of understanding. To the inimitable Kimmy Beach, thank you for your editing expertise and instinct for the heart of a story. And gratitude to Laura Trunkey for an early edit of the developing manuscript.

Thank you so much to David Greer and the close attention of several more devoted reader-editors who shone a light on many of these stories and suggested improvements. I could not have done it without you. To all the women in my poetry group(s), thank you for your support and valuable feedback on my writing and for inspiring me with the creative risks you take in your work. And to my eagle-eyed philosopher who parsed between and amidst the lines to help me find my voice, thank you for your masterful mind and artistic sensibility, and for never doubting I could do this.

To *Geist* editors AnnMarie MacKinnon and Michal Kozlowski, and to *Don't Talk to Me About Love* editors Sam Hiyate and Diane Terrana, thank you for championing my work.

And special gratitude to author Barbara Gowdy, whose short-story collection *We So Seldom Look on Love* inspired me so many years ago, and whose generous reference started me on my submission journey and ultimately toward publication.

I am grateful to the British Columbia Arts Council for a Project Assistance Grant for Creative Writers and to Banff Centre for Arts and Creativity for a Leighton Studios Residency that allowed me to complete the manuscript.

Versions of these stories first appeared in the following publications:

"Ground Zero/Mastering Surface Tension," in *Geist*, Issue 114 Winter

"Belly-Deep in White Clover," in *Prairie Fire* Love Issue, Vol. 39 No. 1

"Velvet Voice," in *Don't Talk to Me About Love* magazine, 2018

"The Collector/So Sorry for Your Loss," in *Kaaterskill Basin Literary Journal*, 2016

"Night People," in *The New Quarterly*, Issue 130

Awards and Nominations:

"Mastering Surface Tension" won the 2017 Writers' Union of Canada Short Prose Competition, and as "Ground Zero" was a Fiction Finalist in the 43rd National Magazine Awards (nominated by *Geist* magazine).

"Velvet Voice" was nominated by *Don't Talk To Me About Love* magazine for the 2019 Writers' Trust/McClelland & Stewart Journey Prize.

"Belly-Deep in White Clover" was longlisted for the 2018 Commonwealth Short Story Prize.

About the Author

ERIN CLAYTON PHOTOGRAPHY

Barbara Black writes fiction, flash fiction and poetry. Her work has been published in Canadian and international magazines, including *The Cincinnati Review*, *The New Quarterly*, *CV2*, *Geist* and *Prairie Fire*. She was recently a finalist in the 2020 National Magazine Awards; was nominated for the 2019 Writers' Trust/McClelland & Stewart Journey Prize; and won the 2017 Writers' Union of Canada Short Prose Competition. She lives in Victoria, BC.